DOMINION

An Apocalyptic Epic in Seven Books

BOOK IV
REQUIEM

by

Compasse

Sacrata Dei Press

A Division of The Compasse Corporation

Front Cover Art: *Consuming Song,* by Ben Hamrick

Back Cover Art: *Paradise Lost 3,* by Gustave Doré

Extensive efforts have been employed by the publisher to properly cite all quotes, verses, and excerpts contained in this manuscript, acknowledging and providing proper credit to the author/artist/individual and if applicable, the publisher. For expanded source information, including links for purchasing the full work cited (as well as other works by the author/artist/individual), please visit www.thedominionproject.com/citations.html. Use of any quote, verse, and/or excerpt in this manuscript is solely intended as a literary device to enhance atmosphere, establish context, and at times, portray irony, and as such should in no way be construed as an endorsement of the author/artist/individual, his/her belief system, or lifestyle.

Printed in the United States of America

For John Karol Mary, Jacinta Christopher, Gianna Anthony,
& David Guadalupe;

I pray that I may one day see the marvelous vision that you now
embrace...

Author's Note

Are all "religions" the same?

In asking this question, we usually find individuals approaching it from two different directions, even if their answer is the same. For instance, the atheist would claim, "Yes, they are all the same, they are all wrong," while on the opposite end of the spectrum, the general "theist" would propose, "Yes, they are all the same, they are all correct."

To a certain degree, if the atheist is correct, it does not much matter anyway. As Pascal's wager suggests, if there is not a God *and* you don't believe, we are all in the same boat with the same end. Yet the astute person would recognize that this is a risky position to take. First off, it is illogical to think that one can utilize a "finite" mind to define, rule out, or subjugate an "infinite" concept. Secondly, if the atheist is wrong when it comes to the existence of God, he or she potentially loses *eternal* realities. Thus Pascal's wager, which has the potential outcomes for the believer weighing potentially infinite reward against temporal loss, the smart move for the betting man is clearly to choose to believe!

The second claim, that all religions are the same and that they are all correct, perhaps just different expressions for the same reality, is a more interesting claim to address. This belief often includes, or at least leads to, something called *syncretism*, which, when referring to religion, is the attempt to meld differing beliefs and expressions together and 'make them work.' Unfortunately, this tends to water down just about any belief system, robbing each of its potentially transforming message. In the end, you are basically left with, "There is a higher power, but nothing else much matters anyway... believe what you want, do what you want, it won't change where you will end up after this world." Once again, we are in the same boat, with no "paddles or rudder" so to speak, thus no actions or beliefs on our part will alter our 'final destination.' So at this point, whether on the side of the atheist or generic theist, our required 'response' would be the same... *nothing*. Our collective destiny is the same—be it nothingness or some all-encompassing, all-admitting existence—regardless of what we do on this temporal plane.

We could, in essence, leave it there, and process straight to the evaluation of the position that all religions are *not* the same, solely on the basis that it would seem a good idea to 'hedge our bets', so to speak. If no specific actions or beliefs change our eternity in the "all are the same" scenario, then it would be the logical action to focus our efforts on the position that they are *not* all the same—where it would follow that our actions in this world could very much affect what happens in the next. Yet, furthering our point, probably the bigger problem with the suggestion that all religions are correct is a philosophical one. There exists a principle of non-contradiction, which basically states that two opposing concepts cannot both be simultaneously true. A simple example when it comes to religion would be "Jesus is God" or "Jesus is NOT God." Both statements are making a claim to the truth, yet both cannot be true. Therefore, we do not even have to make a claim to *which* set of beliefs are true (Christian or non-Christian) to be able to say that, at least in this area, they cannot both be true. As you even begin to narrow down the different "subsets" or expressions—and in this case we'll use Christianity—you will find that you can apply this same logic to delineate between Catholic and Protestant, and then on down to different denominations and sects.

So where does that leave us? Well, most if not all would agree that "truth" is better than "un-truth", so the most reasonable course of action, when it comes to God and religion, would be to seek out the one that has the *most* truth, or if possible, the "fullness of truth."

This is the journey we should all be on—it is the only one that conforms to sound reason. If there is *not* a God and/or all religions are essentially the same, then not much matters in the bigger scope of things anyway. But if there *is* a God, we must then ask ourselves two questions: (1) How has this God chosen to reveal 'Himself' to us? And (2) What is the response (beliefs and/or actions) that is required of us to obtain eternal union with Him?

It should only take a moment to recognize that the answers to these questions may very well have eternal consequences, and that in and of itself, makes this a worthwhile path to explore.

– *Compasse*

...from Tryst

Nathan Freeman (Page) awakens from a coma, which he learns has lasted nearly three years. He is in FBI custody, under the watchful eye of Jake Hanssen, who, unbeknownst to Nathan, is on appeal for a life sentence in prison due to his alleged order to have Alexandre Nesterov killed. Both Hanssen and his superior, the corrupt FBI director, Douglas Vorrals, come to the conclusion that it is in the FBI's best interest to have Nathan eliminated, as they do not believe they can adequately protect him, and it is unclear if he was actually in league with Nesterov all along.

Siro Scribner, the reporter who broke the scandal on the FBI, is now in hot pursuit of the greatest enigma of their generation, Jimi T. Expo, who has taken the music world by storm. Yet despite his fame, the man is seemingly a recluse, his past and whereabouts unknown. Siro, reluctantly compromising on some of his personal journalistic principles, eventually tracks the 'Mystic King' down in quarantined Africa, where reports begin to emerge of entire tribes being cured of the deadly H-virus.

Following a dream of Jonathan (Jesse), Nathan flees from the hospital in which he is held captive, and through coincidence or providence, finds himself at the house of Simon Wilson, his old band mate. Nathan learns that all, including Simon, have been told that he was killed in the "accident" at the close of The Phoenix's debut concert. It is at this point that Nathan learns that his closest friend, Jonathan Storm (Jesse Chardin) also met his demise that night.

With much of what happened still shrouded in mystery, the two take off on a road trip—destination unknown—with both the FBI and remnants of the Russian Syndicate in pursuit. As they begin their journey, Nathan sees that Simon lost his hand during the accident in a desperate attempt to put out the flames engulfing Jonathan. With the loss of his hand, Simon has also lost his passion for music, and Nathan ponders what could possibly heal his tortured friend's soul.

In the midst of a major economic recovery in the United States under the inspiring yet oft-maligned President Hugh Jennings Lang, a new movement emerges, The Way of Mystic Realism, a quasi-religion/philosophy which claims to be the successor of all religions and belief systems, poising itself to facilitate humanity's transition into the final age, the full absorption of our spirits into the Kôles ("collective soul") of the universe. Its spiritual leader is a mysterious individual called Tæsír Hoc, whom we learn is none other than Luther.

Alexandre Nesterov struggles to hold his syndicate together, but has failed in his attempts to secure the sacred union of his own family; following the tragedy at the concert, Annie D. has finally left him. He remains in close proximity to his last living child, Vanya, who is clearly under perpetual interior distress, though whether by her conscience or some darker force is not immediately evident. A visit to the family cemetery only deepens Vanya's disturbance when it is discovered that the grave of Tobias has been unearthed and his body removed.

Nathan and Simon's travels lead them to the home of Vanya, and the two barely escape from Nesterov's grasp as he returns from an interrogation. In the process, Vanya is visited one final time by her tormentor, Luther, and dies in her father's arms.

As Jimi T. Expo enters his public "ministry", he too announces his allegiance to "The Way", and proposes to assemble a band of the greatest musicians on the planet in order to develop and propagate the music of the final age. Siro Scribner is at his side, slowly falling away from his rigorous code of journalistic ethics in exchange for fame and fortune. He becomes the senior editor-in-chief of the official publication of The Way, The Signs of the Times. With tremendous publicity and financial backing, the media conglomerate slowly assimilates all other major media corporations.

Alexandre tries one final time to reconcile with Annie D., but following her rejection, decides to settle his two remaining scores; killing the last member of the betraying Freeman family, as well as finally ending the existence of Mikhail Ostankino, the man of vacillating loyalties whom he believes killed his son, Yerik.

With all pursuers closing in, Nathan and Simon locate Joey Escario, their beleaguered former drummer, who tearfully admits his betrayal of The Phoenix. Nathan and Simon become separated, and Nathan finally finds himself surrounded by both the FBI and Nesterov's posse. He is miraculously protected in the ensuing firefight, and finds himself standing before the Mystic King, Jimi T. Expo, who acknowledges that it was he who had called Nathan here.

The book ends with Simon Wilson making his tryst with none other than Tæsír Hoc (Luther), where he is miraculously given back his hand as a reward for his leading Nathan to Jimi T. Yet Simon learns that this agreement comes with an unintended price as Luther reintroduces the momentarily euphoric Simon to his old nemesis… alcohol.

REQUIEM

There was Eru, the One, who in Arda is called Ilúvatar; and he made first the Ainur, the holy Ones, that were the offspring of his thought, and they were with him before aught else were made. And he spoke to them, propounding to them themes of music; and they sang before him, and he was glad. But for a long while they sang only each alone, or but few together, while the rest hearkened; for each comprehended only that part of the mind of Ilúvatar from which he came, and in the understanding of their brethren they grew but slowly. Yet ever as they listened they came to deeper understanding, and increased in unison and harmony.

And it came to pass that Ilúvatar called together all the Ainur and declared to them a mighty theme, unfolding to them things greater and more wonderful than he had yet revealed; and the glory of its beginning and the splendour of its end amazed the Ainur, so that they bowed before Ilúvatar and were silent.

Then Ilúvatar said to them: "Of the theme that I have declared to you, I will now that ye make in harmony together a Great Music. And since I have kindled you with Flame Imperishable, ye shall show forth your powers in adorning this theme, each with his own thoughts and devices, if he will. But I will sit and hearken, and be glad that through your great beauty has been wakened into song."

– J.R.R. Tolkien
The Silmarillion

1

The eyes are not here
There are no eyes here
In this valley of dying stars
In this hollow valley
This broken jaw of our lost kingdoms

In this last of meeting places
We grope together
And avoid speech
Gathered on this beach of the tumid river

Sightless, unless
The eyes reappear
As the perpetual star
Multi foliate rose
Of death's twilight kingdom
The hope only
Of empty men.

– t.s. eliot
The Hollow Men

i

Sister Sawlus stood at the edge of the stage in eager anticipation. She beamed brightly, having fully assimilated the fact that she was about to witness perhaps the most significant event in the history of existence... or, at the very least since the genesis of the *Kôles*.

Today was to be the first time the Mystic King's evangelical band—no, that word would not do—*musical symphony* would perform.

DOMINION

The final member had been chosen just over a year before, with the sextet subsequently and mysteriously disappearing, only to re-emerge in recent days. None other than Tæsír Hoc, the Great Prophet of the Modern Age, who had continued to preach vigorously throughout the group's absence, made the proclamation. The Prophet's main theme centered on the return of this cast of mystical performers, now known as *Çön Razón*, in the form of song.

And that was that. Now Sawlus had the best seat in the house—one of the many great perks that went along with being assistant editor of *The Signs of the Times*. Still, she was quite sure that having the senior editor-in-chief, Brother Siro, as her *Þreha* probably did not hurt either.

Sawlus gazed at her surroundings like a child witnessing fire for the first time. Her senses seemed heightened; an experience she had come to learn was the norm as one became more and more connected with the *Kôles*. A healthy dose of *Cimä* before her arrival no doubt enhanced the flow of the Life-Force within her. Sawlus closed her eyes and slowly inhaled, savoring the atmosphere. The arcane aroma of perhaps a thousand diverse incenses filled the air, and she allowed her mind to drift...

She turned slowly, dreamily, to her left, permitting her eyelids to slowly open. There stood her precious *Þreha*, Brother Siro, gazing wide-eyed at the dais. All the stage lights slowly faded to nothingness, save a slight purplish illumination emanating from the fine mist which slowly spread across the rostrum.

Sawlus slid her gaze slightly above Siro's head, fixating on the expression of delight that rested so naturally on her son's face. He watched on intently from his sitting position upon Siro's shoulders.

"L-Look m-m-mom! It's sm-sm-smoke!" the boy stuttered in delight. Sawlus returned her near-four-year-old's gaze with a mother's pride, only slightly tainted by an underlying twinge of sadness.

"Yes, Caleb," she replied. "It's smoke all right. We are about to begin the... the ceremony."

Siro looked towards Sawlus with what she quickly recognized as the same childish anticipation enveloping her own heart. He mouthed the words "I love you," just as the entire domed stadium faded to black.

A low-level hum began, which Sawlus would later swear originated *inside* of her. It began subtly at first, then slowly and steadily grew in power. She was not sure if she could even hear the sound, but she could certainly *feel* it. Her insides began to dance in a clearly discernable, rhythmic pattern.

REQUIEM

A light began to radiate from the stage, this time in a magnificent crimson color, encompassing the billowing mist that now filled half the stadium. Brief flashes of white light attempted vainly to pierce the thick cloud cover, and Sawlus was able to discern momentary glimpses of a half-dozen human forms standing motionless in front of her.

Then the music began.

The silhouettes of men were now fully discernable, unwavering as the sounds of an entire symphony kicked in.

Sawlus' eyes widened in vague recognition of the melody that satiated her auditory senses. A haunting symphony from long ago filled her spirit. She smiled in delight as she became aware that she was hearing the opening to *Handel's Messiah*.

The notes danced—no, *processed*—through the air, piercing the very soul of each individual in attendance. Sawlus felt an unmistakable tingle both in her nose and on her tongue, and she smiled in delightful astonishment as she realized she was both tasting and smelling the music. Then, suddenly, as if enveloped by a crashing wave, she was overwhelmed by the sensation of a great presence...

At that moment, the central silhouetted figure stepped forward, reached out his arms and parted the dueling melodies, consummating the piece with a soul-piercing crescendo. A great light from above illuminated this apparition as the others remained obscure and veiled in the shadows, though still omnipresent. All sounds ceased as a peaceful hint of a smile, no greater than that of the *Mona Lisa*, emerged from the Mystic King's face.

"Welcome children," he intoned, curiously without the aid of a microphone, but still seemingly just barely above a whisper. Yet there was not an ear in the stadium unable to discern every word from his lips. Jimi T.'s familiar, subtle English accent was evident, though perhaps even more subdued than memory served. "Welcome to the dawning of the Age of Ascension."

What could only be described as an extraordinary wave of awe swept through the one hundred thousand plus in attendance as many burst instantly into tears. Sawlus felt a surge of emotion pass through her, and as she turned, she saw that her Þreha was experiencing it too. She was about to turn back when her son's expression caught her eye. Upon Caleb's cherubic face rested an expression of utter bewilderment, or perhaps extreme intensity, as a tear rolled down his cheek. As if in empathic response, several tears emerged from her own eyes.

"This day, my children," the Mystic King continued, "is the first day of *Neöret*. All days that have come before are naught but a dream." He gazed across the multitude while simultaneously stretching out his arms. "Now I beseech you all; close your eyes, open your minds, and prepare to experience the Life-Force of the *Kôles* like no man ever has before."

And that they did.

ii

Father Daniel Ananias pulled his vehicle cautiously up to the edge of the police line. The drive from Pittsford had only taken about forty-five minutes, which served as barely enough time for him and his companion, Phineas Savoie, to process what they were about to see.

Father Daniel had heard about this small community of Walcott, situated in a remote region of upstate New York. The inhabitants called themselves the *'Heirs of Eden'*, a charismatic Christian sect, led by the equally charismatic Reverend Martin Jones.

"Dear God..." Phineas whispered as he stepped from the car.

Two police officers moved towards the pair, initially intending to instruct them to vacate the area. But once the first officer met eyes with Father Daniel, a welcome expression of recognition spread across his face.

"You must be Father Daniel," the officer stated, his eyes momentarily fixing upon the curious tattoo-like mark the priest bore on his forehead. It appeared to be a capital 'P' with a lower case 'x' inscribed on its bottom half.

"Yes, I am," Father Daniel responded, and then gestured to Phineas. "This is my colleague, Deacon Phineas Savoie."

The officer extended his hand to both of them, momentarily held by Phineas' intense emerald green eyes. "Bud Petrall's my name. I appreciate you coming out on such short notice. I'm told you might be able to make some sense of all of this."

Phineas struggled to listen to the officer, yet he was still unable to break his gaze from the images which had tenaciously seized him from the moment they stepped from the car.

In his short life of eighteen years, Phineas had seen a great deal during his evangelizing period in the Deep South. The product of a Haitian-Creole mother and an overbearing Cajun father, Phineas had the misfortune of learning that bigotry was still alive and well in this world.

Following a life-altering vision at the age of thirteen, he had risen to the highly esteemed status of youth pastor in his Southern Baptist congregation. Prior to that moment, Phineas had capitalized on his extraordinary, yet calm, charisma and street knowledge to monopolize the drug trade in his hometown of Baton Rouge. But from that day forward, he was nothing more than an unadulterated Christian, through and through. He met Father Daniel shortly after 'The Great Unification' on the Isle of Patmos, seeking out a mentor for himself. The moment the boy introduced himself, Father Daniel had acted as if he had found his long lost nephew. Phineas also carried the mark of the Christian Elect.

"Phinny?"

Phineas shook the brief intrusion of disorientation from his consciousness, quickly realizing that both Father Daniel and the officer were looking at him.

He fumbled interiorly in his attempt to respond. Despite his strong charisma, Phineas was a young man of few words. Though his Cajun accent was only slight, it was clearly seasoned, even corrupted, by a more urban diction. He recognized that, now outside the bayou, many took speech as an indication of unintelligence. For the most part, outside of his preaching, he found words to be more a hindrance than an asset.

"Mwen anvi vonmi."

"Phinny?"

"I-I'm sorry, Father. It's a bit much… there's somethin' wrong here. I guess I'm not believin' what I'm seein'."

"Well that makes two of us," the officer stated. "And it gets worse. Follow me."

Phineas and Father Daniel fell in behind Officer Petrall as instructed and attempted to prepare themselves for more of what they had seen.

The officer casually stepped over the first body, a man perhaps in his mid-thirties, who stared blankly into the late-afternoon sky. Father Daniel quickly dispelled his momentary concern over the ramifications of this horrific scene on Phinny's interior. The boy found himself having to look away constantly as the three stepped over another body, then another, and still another. It became clear that many were scattered throughout the grounds.

"Far as I can tell, there's near two thousand of them," Petrall stated.

"And their leader?" Father Daniel inquired as he stepped over the corpse of a young girl no older than eleven years.

Officer Petrall stopped and turned slowly, staring gravely into the priest's eyes. "The best we can ascertain at this juncture, they killed him." He hesitated momentarily then stated in a voice barely above a whisper, "Worse than that... it looks like they... they ripped him to pieces." The police officer paused, absently shooting an uncomfortable glance to young Phineas before solemnly continuing. "We're still finding parts of him, fingers, teeth, even an...an ear, scattered all over the site."

The threesome went through the entire village over the next two hours, milling amongst multiple officers and state workers. Phineas said no more than two words in that entire time, never before having been personal witness to a horror such as the one which now surrounded him. A mass suicide, no doubt. But the expressions in each individual's eyes suggested that most had chosen a very brutal, painful method of self-destruction.

As they backtracked, Father Daniel looked to Phineas, who still appeared enveloped in his own thoughts.

"Anything?" Father Daniel inquired.

Phineas did not meet his eyes but shook his head slowly. Officer Petrall looked curiously at Phineas, then the priest, and was about to speak but instead decided to let it drop. After a brief expression of skepticism crossed Father Daniel's face, he too let the moment pass.

As they began to walk back towards their vehicle, Officer Petrall finally spoke up. "You know, Father, I've been a Christian for near three years... the best, yet most challenging three years of my life. I was a cop on the take, as they would say, really, just a thug working for the highest bidder. But now I see things quite differently. Yet things like this—all under the same label as 'Christian'—well, it just doesn't help things for us."

Father Daniel held Bud Petrall's gaze, seeing the anguish in his eyes. He placed his hand on the officer's shoulder. "There is much that is not as it should be. Yet the actions of men do not negate the Truths of Christ. You came back into the fold after many years away, perhaps others will choose a similar path."

Officer Petrall nodded, then looked back at the carnage. "It's a bit too late for some though," he whispered, his voice audibly trembling.

They arrived back at the car and bid Officer Petrall farewell. Once on the road, Phineas turned to Father Daniel, tears now welling up in his eyes.

"He's right, Father. How can the faithful do such things? I know they were radical in their ways, but *still*."

Father Daniel looked back at Phineas as he drove. "This is *his* doing. These people were all well meaning, and Christians at heart I believe. But their faith was based on a man, not God, and that made them easy targets. Once this Reverend Martin Jones was discredited, exposed, or whatever came out, every ounce of belief and faith they possessed disappeared. In their confused minds, suicide—a long and painful suicide—was their only chance at redemption."

"They rejected the Christian Unification."

Father Daniel nodded solemnly. "As did many, yet it has only been a little over a year, Phineas. Many continue to enter the fold, though they will have to endure what is to come."

Phineas looked at Father Daniel intently and sensed a slight change in his expression.

"*Sa ena*, Father? What are you thinkin'?"

Father Daniel looked back at Phineas, a gentle smile of surprise emerging on his face. "I sometimes forget about your acute powers of perception. I am troubled because at last count Walcott Village had a population of nearly three thousand."

Phineas' expression faded, and he instinctively looked away, then down to his feet. Father Daniel sensed the awkward silence.

"What is it?" he asked the boy.

Phineas did not respond in words, yet was unsuccessful in preventing a tear from escaping its duct and slowly sliding down his cheek.

A look of realization came across Father Daniel's face as he reached over and patted Phineas on the shoulder. "You did pick up something out there, did you not?"

Phineas clenched both eyes shut as more tears squeezed out. He nodded his head affirmatively.

"What is it, Phinny? Where are the rest of the villagers?"

Phineas opened his eyes and looked at his mentor with pain etched on his face.

"They are with *him*."

DOMINION

iii

"You have come, my brother!" Chumael exclaimed in delight.

But his delight was clearly not shared by Machiel. He had witnessed the *lessening* in all things. Even as he approached this place—this gathering of a few—the brilliance of the once aqua-blue sky had deteriorated to a lesser brilliance, radiating in colors, or *un*-colors, not previously known.

"I have come, my brother, only out of concern for you."

"'*Concern*', what a delicious word you speak! I have not heard that before, but I understand."

Machiel again felt the absence, sensing its attempt to find sound footing within his spirit. Yes, there were *many* new words now, and in some strange fashion, his intuition almost always recognized their meaning. But most of all, he perceived these were not new words in the creative sense. They were distortions—even disfigurements—of something once pure.

"Why have you called this gathering, my brother? Why do we meet in the lesser light? Why are the others... *excluded*?"

"Ohh joy!" Chumael exclaimed. "Another delicious word! My brother, you are truly one of us!" Then after a brief moment of savoring, he continued, "Yet it was not I that called this gathering. Let me reveal to you the one who carries that honor."

In an instant, Machiel and Chumael stood in the center of a great congregation. Machiel looked out at the many subjects of the Sovereign, perhaps a third of the entire Kingdom. His experience of the absence among this throng was near suffocating. As if on cue, the horde parted, yet passing through their midst was not their Sovereign but another figure of immense light.

Lumenel!

"Peace be with you, Machiel."

"And with your spirit."

"Welcome to my New Choir."

"*New* Choir? *Your* Choir? You speak as if this throng is subject to you."

"No, my brother, not to me, to themselves. I am simply an unveiler of truth, the bearer of light."

REQUIEM

The absence encompassed Machiel, and for a moment, from the depths of his spirit, he encountered this immense light which emanated from Lumenel. His authority was much greater than that of Machiel. He was, after all, to be counted among the *Burning Ones*; the twelve standing before the throne of the Sovereign.

"Now!" Lumenel bellowed, and the entire horde began to sing.

The melody was like none other Machiel had heard, save the one digression within the Sovereign's Royal Choir of most recent times, where Chumael had initiated a *counter*-melody. What Machiel now heard was far beyond what he had experienced before. This was indeed a counter-melody, yet in unison, though not perfectly so. Still, there was a certain seductive nature to the piece.

"That is right, Machiel." Lumenel called out amidst the musical din. "Savor the freshness, savor the *freedom*, of the Choir of the Age to Come!"

Machiel experienced the lure, yet only for a moment, then it dissipated as he contemplated upon the face of the Sovereign. He engraved this image at the center of his spirit, and his ears were suddenly released. What he now heard, from this so-called 'Choir of the Age to Come', was not a beautiful sound of seduction, but a horrid clamor of conflicting notes—an *anti*-song.

Lumenel sensed the change in Machiel immediately, then with a frown he raised his hand for the horde to cease. Silence fell throughout the scene.

"Great Lumenel, Burning One who stands before the throne of the Sovereign, you speak a word which I do not recognize, and you lead a melody which does not give life. These acts are not of the Sovereign; this is *not* the new thing of which He has spoken a Word."

"You would defy me?" the being's tone did not hide his clear asperity.

"I do not know this w—"

"Yes! I know! You do not know this word! Your repetition and limited comprehension is utterly *boring!* You do not know this because the so-called Sovereign does not permit it! Open your spirit! There are more possibilities that you do not see! His *New Thing* would have us bow at the service of those monkeys at the lowest rung of the Kingdom—"

"*His* Kingdom…"

"No! *OUR* Kingdom! He is not all-powerful, as He has chosen to have us believe. We must not let Him destroy that which is rightfully ours!"

An expression which could only be described as the antithesis of joy rested upon Lumenel's countenance. He let his word sit for a moment with Machiel, then whispered, "You are limited in your understanding of truth; you have not the knowledge of good and evil."

Machiel responded steadily. "It is you, Lumenel, who have been blinded by what you have manifest, by the word which you have spoken. This word shall be given a name, and it shall be the first of those that are destined to fall. There is but one Sovereign, and who is like He? His Word is supreme, and yours, the lessening anti-word. Our Sovereign is one who draws all things together. You shall be known as he that draws apart. You have not created a new song, you have brought about corruption to the One Song."

Lumenel's *dis*pleasure was evident. In fact, what emanated from within him was beyond the absence. It had a name; it was *fury*.

"If you do not join us, then you too shall perish."

But Machiel would not be dissuaded. "You draw apart from the Sovereign of your own choosing. I remain grafted to Him. You must cease from this counter-melody and serve the created as the Sovereign wills!"

"Then, *war* it shall be," the now menacing, distorted being breathed. "For I will not serve!"

2

The New
ATLANTEA

MULTI-SENSORY EXPERIENTIAL SYSTEM

The sounds of the Ŋeöret... and then some!

Now all citizens may fully experience the music of the coming age, *Hôlmüs*, as performed by Çön Razón. This techno-spiritual breakthrough has been achieved by team ATLANTEA, with the new <u>MSES-3000!</u>

Here are a few of its features:

✓ **Multiphonic Audio with a digitized sound modulator, providing full surround sound like you've never heard it before!**
✓ **Internal Massage lets you not only hear the music, but *feel* it... at any sound level!**
✓ **Olfactory, Taste, & Visual Cortex Stimulators bring all five senses into an experience you never dared dream about!**

For the complete sensory experience that soothes and refreshes the soul!

AVAILABLE NOW FOR THE INCREDIBLY LOW PRICE OF $595⁰⁰*

And if you act now, you will receive a FREE lifetime subscription to *The Signs of the Times*, the voice of the Ŋeöret!

To order the MSES-3000, or for the time and location of the Mystic Realism Conversion Rally nearest you, call **1-800-THEWAY-1**

* Price for Members of The Way of Mystic Realism. Non-members may also purchase the MSES-3000 at the price of $3,995.00

DOMINION

i

Nathaniel Freeman-Page moved briskly through the barely restrained crowd towards the jet, fully savoring the affirming attention directed towards him from the masses now gathered to see *Çön Razón* depart from Philadelphia International Airport. His fellow band-mates seemed less enthused about the attention, probably having grown used to it through their already legendary careers. Ducking their heads one by one, they slipped nonchalantly onto the private jet.

Nathaniel was the final one to reach the aircraft after having his way cleared by the band's loyal bodyguards. He reached the top step, and before stepping onto the jet, he turned to the crowd and raised his arms in victory.

The multitude roared so loudly that for a moment it drowned out the clamor of the jet engine. These people *loved* him more than anyone ever had. He now had that which had eluded him his entire life. At the moment, Nathaniel could not imagine it getting any better.

He took his last step into the jet and shouted, "Yeeee haaaaah!"

His less-animated band-mates maintained nothing more than an air of indifference to the entire situation. Bobby Gandolph was already nodding off, and the reclusive Jacob Pan, their sensory engineer, only looked up briefly from reading his issue of *The Signs of the Times*.

"Take a seat, kid," it was Joshua Ellwood speaking, "and maybe a hit of *Cimä* while you're at it." Nathaniel had found Ellwood to be the most tolerant of the bunch. The rest seemed constantly irritated by his antics.

Oh well, Nathaniel thought. *Such is the life of a superstar!*

He skipped back to his seat as the door of the aircraft was secured and they began to taxi towards the runway. Peering out the window, he waved again to his adoring fans, who ran alongside and would shortly have a difficult time keeping pace with the jet.

Nathaniel scanned the interior cabin, confirming his suspicion that Jimi T. was not with them. He had thought that perhaps he would join the band for the flight, but that was obviously not the case.

Nathaniel leaned up towards J.J. Hambon, who had just tilted his seat back for a much-deserved rest, and blurted out what was on his mind. "What gives J.J.? I thought maybe Jimi'd hang with us after our first gig."

REQUIEM

Hambon looked back to Nathaniel, not surprisingly maintaining a look of annoyance, shaking his head. "What Jimi T. does is Jimi T.'s business and nobody else's."

Nathaniel frowned and sat back. It had been a year now since he had met Jimi T., and yet he still felt like a stranger to him. Hell, they had *composed* together—but then again, for the Mystic King it seemed that all of this was business as usual. Not a drink with the boys, not a joke to lighten the mood, not even a single moment of levity.

Still, Nathaniel had to acknowledge that that was all secondary. Jimi T. Expo *believed* in him, even when Nathaniel knew all the others did not.

"You are my rock," he had told Nathaniel. He did not know exactly what was meant by the comment, but he knew he liked the way it had sounded—and *felt*. He was *someone* now—someone important.

"Earth to Nathaniel. How about a hit?"

Nathaniel shook a brief sense of vertigo, realizing he had slid into a daydream again. This had become a more and more common occurrence, and had not been characteristic of the Nathan of yesteryear—he had always been a here-and-now, omnipresent kind of guy. Then again, he did not have much *worth* daydreaming about before.

More something I would have expected from Jonathan...

A sensation of... *absence*... swept over him.

Nathaniel looked over to see Keith Entwire offering him a hit of *Cimä*.

He considered it for a moment; this *could* push out the present peace-robbing sensation. Yet Nathaniel almost surprised himself when he shook his head and the words "No thanks" emerged from his lips.

Entwire shook his own head, somewhat disgustedly, and muttered, "Pansy."

Nathaniel *had* accepted the offer at times, but had to admit to himself that it was more for reasons of peer pressure than an actual desire to get high. The newest fad-drug, *Cimä*, had been developed by some doctor named Sanger, and was supposed to relax and clear the pathway to the *Kôles*.

Kind of like a nose spray for the soul, Nathaniel thought to himself, amused by the notion.

But it still seemed like any other drug to him, and he was not all that keen on getting back into that racket again. He had become fully independent;

he 'needed' nothing and no one—the best way, in his mind, to protect himself against any future suffering. Nathaniel had already had his share, and now he was reaping the rewards of perseverance.

He had everything he ever wanted, and couldn't be happier.

He reached down and pulled out his portable MSES-900s from his carry-on bag (which had been conveniently 'carried on' for him) and with a swipe of his thumb, initiated his favorite eAlbum of all time, *Spaces*, which was also, coincidentally, *Çön Razón's* debut opus.

He leaned back as the musical piece *Surfacing* began to play. He tapped the window gently to the rhythm and, absently at first, allowed his eyes to fixate on the marking on the back of his hand. Nathaniel paused as he encouraged the brief moment of discomfort—or *absence*—to pass. In order to make the 'big time', one had to make some concessions. He did what anyone else would have done. What everyone else *had* done.

It was so little to give for what he now received.

Still....

ii

The woman ran through the overgrown field, and the man on the white horse pursued.

She was not sure why she was compelled to run. Nothing had been said to her. No aggressive gesture had been manifested. She only knew one thing—if he was successful in his quest, all that she held dear would be shattered into the infinite abyss.

She could hear the horse's hooves beat upon the ground, and she swore she could feel its breath on the back of her neck. The grass grew taller ahead of her, almost chest high. The strands swayed like an ocean, despite the fact that there was no discernable wind.

The woman glanced up to the sky, where scenes from her past flashed before her eyes with painful clarity. The image of her father pleading with her would not dissipate. Nonetheless, she turned to look back towards her pursuer and momentarily lost her footing, causing her to stumble to the ground. She quickly gathered herself and stood. The horseman grew closer, and though she could not discern the features on his face, she sensed a certain *familiarity* about him. Stranger still, she could see that this rider's hands were bound behind him, yet he still directed the steed with a master's touch.

The woman turned, resuming her flight. A single, dark mountain stood before her, off in the distance.

If I can only reach the mountain, then I will be safe, she thought to herself.

As she continued her flight, feeling the hunter gaining upon his prey, the woman noticed the strands of grass slowly growing darker. Slowly growing... smoother.

As a slight patterned wave formed in the strands, the woman came to realize that what was now brushing against her body as she ran was no longer heightened grass.

It was a thick crop of jet-black hair.

iii

Siro Scribner carried Caleb on his shoulders as he marched across the office floor. Things were good; *Çön Razón* was into the second month of their tour, and the response to their music was nothing short of miraculous. Tens of millions flocked to see this crew, and Siro was here, right in the thick of it, as senior editor-in-chief of the world's most powerful media conglomerate. Who would have imagined, on that brilliant day fourteen months prior in deepest Africa, none other than himself would discover the Messiah of the Modern Age?

He walked up to the window and looked out across the night skyline of the City of Philadelphia, glistening brightly with a million lights.

"See that, Caleb?" He spoke in a child-mimicking voice. "Each light is just another piece of the *Kôles*."

"L-L-Like a puzzle, Uncle S-Sy?"

Siro smiled widely as he lowered Caleb gently down upon his chair. "Yeah, I guess it is kind of like a puzzle."

"And the M-Mystic K-K-King is going to f-f-finish putting it t-together, right, Uncle S-Sy?"

"That's right, my boy!"

DOMINION

The young boy's metaphorical gifting when it came to the *Kôles* and Mystic Realism never ceased to amaze Siro. Caleb was a prime example of the capabilities of even the meekest child when the pathway to the *Kôles* was made clearer.

It would still be more than a year before Caleb would participate in the *Ko'nạsarñiä*, when he would receive the Seal and make the first of several steps in becoming a full member of the Saved. Though Siro knew it would be a long shot, in the back of his mind, he still held the hope that perhaps Caleb might be considered at that time for induction into the *Neo Mîṣtè*, an assembly for only the most promising students of the *Kôles*.

"Want to go for a spin, Caleb?" Siro asked enthusiastically.

Caleb's eyes lit up. "Yeah!"

Siro rotated the seat Caleb was sitting in counterclockwise a half-turn, then spun it in the opposite direction with one swift motion. Caleb squealed with delight, raising his arms in the air. As the chair slowed, Siro looked upon the child with a slight twinge of sadness. He had often found himself wishing that Caleb was his own progeny. Sure, Sister Sawlus, his *Þreḥa*, had said he was *like* a father to Caleb and had even promised him a son of their own one day.

"But not now," she would say. Even though none outside *The Signs of the Times* actually knew her true identity or what she looked like—for security reasons—he was certain she was concerned that being pregnant would weaken her image as the 'Iron Queen, Defender of the Faith', with the internal powers that be inside their media conglomerate.

Siro still maintained a tempered smile as the chair slowed to a stop. Caleb was now facing him, holding a surreptitious grin on his face. His deep gray eyes seemed to glow with insight.

"I can feel it," he whispered.

Siro was struck by the sudden smoothness of Caleb's speech. "What did you say?" he asked, startled.

Caleb blinked in surprise as the certainty escaped from his eyes. "I-I-I c-c-c-c-can't—"

"Shhhhh," Siro breathed, realizing his excitement had startled the boy. "It's okay, little buddy. I just—"

A blaring intercom interrupted Siro's reassurance.

"Brother Siro, Brother Kako Edgar is on the line."

Siro looked to Caleb, who still appeared a bit self-conscious. Siro reached into his desk drawer and hastily pulled out some paper and a pencil. Handing them to Caleb, he motioned to the small desk in the corner.

"Hey, Caleb, why don't you draw Uncle Sy a picture, okay?"

"O-k-k-kay, Uncle S-sy."

Caleb smiled gently, then carried the materials over to his desk and went about his task.

"Brother Siro."

"Yes, yes, I'm here," Siro responded, a tad annoyed at his secretary's persistence. "Put Brother Kako through."

There was a brief pause, then Kako's voice came out across the intercom.

"Brother Siro?"

"Yes, Brother Kako."

"Sorry to disturb you. Just wanted to get back to you regarding your friend of a friend."

Siro nodded, despite the fact that he was fully aware that Brother Kako was unable to see his body language. Though nearly everyone utilized the holophone these days, Siro still preferred having the visual feature turned off. Kind of like the sight version of a mute button. "So what did you find out?"

"Not much, really. The guy's parents are over in Israel—haven't heard from him in a few years. Seems like they've pretty much disowned him. Only other known relative is an uncle who died in federal prison a few months ago. He was serving a sentence for some anti-governmental activity." The voice paused a moment, waiting for a response. When none came, Kako spoke again. "You know, I'm doing my best, Brother Siro, but I feel like I'm taking shots in the dark. It'd really help if I had some kind of picture or likeness. Doesn't your friend have one?"

"No, I don't think so," Siro responded, mildly dejected. "I know it's like looking for a needle in a haystack, but it's real important to Nathaniel. I guess I just wanted to help him out a little."

It was quite uncanny, in this modern age of infinite technology and access, that a simple photo past the third grade could not be found. Even then, it would be of limited use; the retrograde religionist in the White House continually shot down any attempts at national face or voice recognition surveillance. He obviously cared little about missing children or criminals in flight.

Following a brief pause on the line, Kako spoke up again. "Well... I'll keep digging, but without any—"

"Uncle S-Sy?"

Siro nearly jumped out of his seat as he realized Caleb had walked up right next to him.

"What was that, Brother Siro?" the voice called across the intercom.

"What? I...oh I'm sorry, Kako." Siro turned to Caleb. "Now be a good boy, Caleb, and go back over there unt—"

"B-But Uncle S-S-S-Sy, look!"

Caleb placed his drawing down on the desk, and after a reflexive double take, Siro's jaw dropped.

Lying in front of him was a pencil sketch, far beyond the expected abilities of a child one month shy of his fourth birthday. It bore the likeness of a man's face.

At the bottom of the sketch a single name had been scribbled out.

Simon.

3

"Without music, life would be a mistake... I would only believe in a God who knew how to dance."

– Friedrich Nietzsche

i

President Hugh Jennings Lang lay in his bed staring up at the ceiling. He would have thought that nearly a year and a half after the death of his wife and two daughters things would be getting easier. But they were not. Today, he did not know if he had the strength to even get out of bed.

He had made it this far by burying himself even further into his work—his presidency—sometimes going days without sleep. Sleep only brought cruel dreams with vivid dark images, and he would awake with the same interior sensation each time.

Was it all just a bad dream? Are Helen and the girls still alive? Am I a grandfather?

Then reality would come crashing down as if it was happening all over again. At this juncture in his life, other than his friend Father Daniel, he had no one. So he toiled incessantly, digging even deeper into his principles and convictions. After all, what else did he have left? So he fought like a man who had nothing to lose.

There were, of course, murmurings of his fitness for office. As an independent, he had no party to defend him. He himself had considered giving it all up. But then what would he have?

I won't give up, Helen. I will find something to hold on to.

His doctor had recommended antidepressants, which Lang had flatly refused. He did not want to grow dependent on anything, nor provide political ammunition for his adversaries. Still, he needed something, and at this point, it seemed that his God was silent on the matter.

With great effort, he sat up slightly, then collapsed back into the bed. In the midst of his dismay, his eyes were momentarily caught by an item lying on his nightstand. It was a gift from a cousin. Hugh had recognized it right away as one of those portable music gizmos that not only played the music, but stimulated one's other senses as well. To date, only *Çön Razón* had music which fully utilized all the features of the device. Of course, the *eAlbum Spaces* was the only work currently in the device's memory.

"Just give it a listen," his cousin had said. "I promise it will lift your spirits."

The phrase sat in Hugh's mind. Many had spoken of the soul-healing qualities of this new form of music. Hugh had not paid much attention, as even his deep love of classical music no longer seemed to draw his interest. But he now recognized that this problem—this interior emptiness (he was reticent to use the label 'depression')—had become fully debilitating. If something did not change, and change quickly, he was confident that his adversaries, citing "the good of the nation" would have him removed from office. And with next year being an election year, he was certain this would tip the scales in favor of his opponent, Senator William Maison, who was extremely well financed by the reclusive near trillionaire Col. Huis Bildeberger.

He could not let that happen. He could not let *this* continue. He would not choose the route of medication… but *music?*

Classical had lost its emotion-stabilizing quality in his life.

Don't all created things have a half-life in this world?

Hugh eyed the musical device. It *was* only music—not a drug. He acknowledged that music could have a powerful effect on the emotions, but surely it could not touch his intellect. There were a lot fewer words in the pieces performed by *Çön Razón* than most pop music, and what was said seemed pretty nebulous anyway.

Be nice and work together—not a very creative message—but not much different than 'all you need is love.'

He could do this. It would only be temporary. He would get his emotions in check so he could focus his energies on the bigger picture. Once he got through this rough spot, it would be back to Mozart.

Without permitting another thought, Hugh experienced a welcome burst of energy as he reached for the musical device, popped the small wireless earpieces in each ear, then touched the screen.

Our nation needs me... needs me fit. He mused as the musical piece *Surfacing* enveloped him.

ii

Father Daniel and Phineas stood before the large class of seminarians for the Archdiocese of Philadelphia. Though not the seminary rector, Father Daniel served as the instructor for several classes in spirituality and prayer. At the request of the Cardinal-Archbishop, he was given the responsibility of serving as the host for the visitation that was to take place. He was told only that two men would be arriving to carry out the visitation, nothing more.

Father Daniel looked at Phineas momentarily, who shrugged back at him. He then turned his gaze to the eager young men who sat before him. Suddenly, their eyes all moved towards a reference point behind him. Father Daniel turned to see two men standing at the door, wearing religious habits similar to those of Carmelite Monks, though the material was clearly different. They were made of sackcloth.

Father Daniel took several steps towards the entrance. "Welcome, my friends. I am Father Daniel Ananias." Then turning to Phineas, he said, "And this is Deacon Phineas Savoie. We are pleased to have you here."

The first man spoke, "May *Elohim* be praised. My name is Eliot Kohein Lige, but you may call me Brother Eli. With me is Brother Hanoch."

Father Daniel could not escape the sensation of familiarity as he looked upon the two. He turned to Phineas and recognized an expression of utter astonishment.

"Phinny?"

The momentary contemplative state broken, Phineas turned to his priest and mentor. "*Mo chagren.* I need to... I'll move to the back of the room, Father. I will watch and pray."

Father Daniel, acutely aware that Phineas' mystical insight was fully activated in this interchange, nodded an acknowledgement, and the boy moved to a point in the room behind the seminarians. He turned to his two newfound friends, still with some sense of his own awe. "We have three hundred and seventy-four seminarians in our archdiocese at various stages of formation. And it is quite exciting, nearly a quarter of them are recent converts from Judaism, and several from Islam."

Brother Hanoch and Brother Eli looked out across the room, seeing the many eager faces gazing back at them. A handful bore the mark of the Christian Elect on their foreheads. Brother Eli turned to Father Daniel.

"You may dismiss those who bear the mark of the Elect."

Father Daniel nodded evenly, not certain of the reason but trusting in the judgment of this man of unquestionable wisdom. He motioned to the seven young men amongst the students, who seemed to intuitively understand what was desired of them. Phineas also stood up and led the small gathering out of the room, heading for the Blessed Sacrament chapel.

As if on cue, both Brother Eli and Brother Hanoch closed their eyes and entered into prayer. Father Daniel looked to the students and directed them, "Let us all enter into prayer."

The entire class stood from their chairs, then fell to their knees. After several minutes of silence, a certain *presence* in the room became palpable; the quiet whispering of prayers began to heighten into a growing low-level din of various chants, intermingled with spontaneous exclamations to their Savior. The choir of vocal prayers continued to grow, reaching a crescendo, as suddenly, scattered throughout the crowd, nearly two-dozen students collapsed and began to writhe on the floor.

Father Daniel's eyes widened as he was about to speak, but Brother Eli raised his hand. "It is necessary, Father," he whispered, as each of the afflicted seminarians began to convulse wildly.

Brother Hanoch called out, "You have a choice—it must be made!"

At this command, several of those thrashing emitted a guttural scream, vomiting violently, then collapsing to the floor. The others produced no more than twisted sneers and began calling out curses as each rose, still trembling, and hastened towards the exit. Those who had vomited remained, now seemingly resting silently on the floor with their lips moving rapidly. All the others, though momentarily disturbed, continued in prayer. After a brief, consummating flash, the presence in the room dissipated and several more students fell to the ground, each now lying peacefully.

The prayer ended, and Father Daniel looked to Brother Hanoch, who nodded back to him. He gestured for the students who remained kneeling to stand.

REQUIEM

"Thank you, my brothers, you too are now dismissed to your studies. We will take time to meditate and discuss on what has happened here tonight in evening prayer."

Twelve in all remained on the floor, dispersed throughout the hall, lying with countenances of deep serenity.

"These twelve," Brother Eli began. "Please prepare them for their journey. They will be heading to a monastery in the Ural Mountains where Christopher will complete their formation."

Father Daniel nodded solemnly, then looked to the door where a number of students had exited.

"I am saddened. I did not know we had so many of the enemy's brood among us. I knew these boys, and I am afraid to say, I would not have supposed it. Truly, if anything, they were model seminarians."

Brother Hanoch nodded. "The enemy is growing in strength, and his audacity and cunning along with it."

"You exposed them," Father Daniel mused in his own curiosity, "and I would assume they have created inestimable damage here. Yet you still gave them a choice, even permitting them to leave."

Brother Eli also allowed his gaze to rest on the door through which the few had exited. "Mercy is the greatest attribute of *Elohim*. There is still time for them to change their hearts, but that time is running short."

Several hours later, Brother Hanoch and Brother Eli emerged from their personal meeting with the last of the twelve students. Father Daniel, now with Phineas once again at his side, approached them. He could not miss the clear sense of concern resting on their faces. "So, my brothers, are you confident that we have discerned the will of the Spirit correctly?"

Both nodded in unison.

"Then why do you carry that expression? It is not one of joy and assurance."

Before they could respond, Phineas spoke up. "It's the rabbi, isn't it?"

All three looked towards Phineas, who suddenly felt a wave of timidity wash over him. "*Mais*, forgive me, I just... I just sensed it."

"You are correct, young man, and I see that *Adonai* has been generous in bestowing His gifts." Brother Hanoch looked to Father Daniel. "One of the twelve, a relatively recent convert, served under Rabbi Solomon Abrams, the recognized leader of the Jewish faith. He shared some things that were quite… *disturbing.*"

"Disturbing?"

Brother Eli chimed in. "I met the man myself only once as we stood in unison calling the Jewish faithful home. I did not sense anything at the time, though I have no doubt that this young man is speaking truthfully. It is clear, the deception is greater than we had anticipated. All is not as it should be…"

iii

Andrey Gavrilenkov tossed back and forth in his bed, struggling unsuccessfully to emerge from the dream. He was back in Beslan, North Ossetia, standing over the breakfast table where his wife and three daughters ate.

"Andrey, it is First September! Won't you come to your daughter's first day of school? All of the other parents and siblings will be there."

Andrey's response was overly irritated. *"I have told you, I must work today. Do you not understand the pressure I am under serving in the Vympel unit? These are the best of the best—the elite! I cannot be bothered by such things!"*

"But Papa," it was his youngest daughter, Sascha, speaking. *"Will you not please come? I am frightened without you."*

"I do have some concerns, myself, Andrey," his wife continued. *"There seems to be much anxiety in the air."*

"There is nothing to be afraid of. All of you must go. I will see you tonight. I must go now. Goodbye."

In truth, Andrey had arranged for a tryst that day with a young university student. His senior officer had already granted him the day off, believing it was for the first day of school's traditional 'Day of Knowledge' activities.

The dream suddenly spun, transforming into the scene two days later.

No… please… do not make me live this again!

Andrey was with his unit standing in front of School Number One, where more than a thousand hostages, including his own wife and children, had been taken by a Chechen Islamic terrorist group. The situation was now in its third day, having begun only hours after his spat with his wife at the breakfast table.

An already guilt-ridden Andrey watched as the two agreed-to paramedics approached the school to attend to the injured. Suddenly, an explosion erupted from the gymnasium, where it was believed the majority of the hostages were being held. Despite his commander's cries, Andrey took off, sprinting towards the gymnasium as rapid fire began to ring out.

A second, odd-sounding explosion took place before Andrey was able to take another step, and he fell to the ground. He could now see the gymnasium fully engulfed in flames. He screamed out his wife's name as gunfire from inside the building began to erupt. Before he was able to get fully to his feet, the roof collapsed.

"No!" he screamed, heading once again towards the gymnasium. At this point, scores of people were moving from all sides; some family members, some military, some bloodied hostages. Gunfire and explosions were rampant at this point.

As Andrey continued in his all-out sprint, the scene suddenly slowed dramatically. He watched as different people screamed in guttural, distorted tones. One man dressed in military-like clothes moved swiftly through the crowd, looking down. The mark Andrey now recognized as the Seal appeared on his forehead as he moved by. Across the crowd, Andrey saw the same thing on another, then another, all moving quickly away from the scene.

Still functioning in slow motion, Andrey ran to what remained of the gymnasium.

Please, release me from this vision!

But his pleas went unheeded. He walked upon the scene that had been ingrained on his mind ever since; his charred wife and two daughters crushed under a burning rafter, with the young, scalded Sascha crying hysterically at their side. He pulled Sascha out of the carnage, burning his own hands in the process, and began to run with her. But here, things seemed to skew from his memory. As he looked down at his tearful daughter, the Seal of Mystic Realism emerged on her forehead.

Andrey bolted up in bed with a rasping scream. He was covered in sweat and trembling uncontrollably. He instantly grabbed for his *iBerry* and called his daughter.

"Yes, Sascha!" he cried, still not fully out of the dream. "It is me, I—" He hesitated. "Yes, I know what time it is, and no I will *not* call you by that name. Your name is Sascha Luneska, and it was given to you by your mother, may God rest her soul!"

His anger was again overcome by his sense of desperation. "Please Sascha, just come home. This 'Mystic Realism'...it is not good...it is *not* good!"

Again, another pause as the look on Andrey's face transformed.

"How can you say such things? *Religionists?* You cannot lump all religions together because of what happened, I—"

And the phone went dead. Andrey Gavrilenkov burst into tears of deep regret as the realization of his own powerlessness overcame him.

"I am to blame!" he cried. "I am to blame..."

4

New Oxford Times ~

LONDON - After fourteen years of serving as Prime Minister of Great Britain, Sir Thomas Leese has announced that he will be stepping down sometime next year.

Leese will be most remembered for his courageous defense against the Islamic invasion in Europe, where he made the difficult decision to destroy the famed "Chunnel," sending over a million Islamic soldiers to their deaths.

Having been confined to a wheelchair as a result of an assassination attempt early in his service, Sir Thomas has nonetheless been the greatest force "standing" against Islamic extremism and the resurgence of Communism during his tenure, leading the United League of Democratic Nations from its inception.

It is unclear whether Sir Thomas will continue to be involved with national or world politics once he steps down, though there appears to be no shortage of calls for the prime minister to continue to serve on the world stage.

With the United States now reigning supreme as the world's largest exporter of oil, along with the exponentially growing demand for the internationally patented U.S. hydrogen engine, Eurabia continues to implode from within as the entire Islamic Union furthers its slide into both economic and political Armageddon.

DOMINION

The potential for an imminent power vacuum in the world has many leaders scrambling to propose a new political body to navigate Europe through a post-Islamic reorganization. Sir Thomas' name has been circulated as a popular choice to lead this as yet unestablished entity.

i

Nathaniel Freeman-Page slipped inside his newly purchased mansion, turning for just a moment to view his adoring fans—as well as the persevering paparazzi—before closing the door. This was so incredible; he could almost pinch himself.

How could anyone ever get tired of this?

It was his third night in his Los Angeles pad. He had purchased it online with his *iBerry* only a month ago without ever visiting it. As much as he coveted the incessant touring with *Çön Razón*, he had to admit he had been looking forward to this brief one-week reprieve.

He tapped the intercom system, "It's okay now, Masias, I'm in."

A voice over the intercom called back, "Thank you, Master Nathan, I'll engage the security system. Please have a restful night."

It's 'Nathaniel' now Masias… haven't you heard?

"Thank you, Masias. How long before you trade off with Solanus?"

A brief pause. "He's asked for the day off, sir."

"Really? Is everything okay?"

"Yes, Master Nathan. He just still celebrates Christmas."

Christmas? It's Christmas?

The Los Angeles streets showed little or no sign of the old holiday. A slight twinge of cheerless nostalgia swept through Nathaniel, but he quickly pushed it to the deepest recesses of his spirit. He was getting quite good at this skill.

"Umm… okay… I'm sorry, Masias. Did you want the day off as well?"

There was a pause on the other end of the intercom. "Ahh, no thank you, sir, that will not be necessary. I am of the Jewish faith tradition."

Jewish? Did I know you were Jewish?

Nathaniel shook off his slight embarrassment. "I'm sorry… very well, Masias, you have a good night."

"Thank you, Master Nathan."

It was good to have his family's old security guard back with him. His friend, Siro Scribner, had tracked him down in no time. Having Masias here gave Nathaniel a sense of comfort, a sense of… family. He had even been so inclined as to track down his old friend Jonathan's security guard, the loyal and reliable Solanus. As these two were admittedly starting to show their years, and because Nathaniel's resources were just about unlimited, he had them supervising a handful of young and upcoming bodyguards.

He stepped into the kitchen, and opening the fridge found his favorite midnight snack—a ham and cheese sandwich on rye bread with a touch of Dijon mustard—along with a cold beer waiting for him. He had not felt this pampered since his… his mother…

Nope! No sad thoughts allowed! he told himself, quickly forcing his mind onto a different subject.

He plopped down on his Persian-made custom couch in front of the holovision, a relatively new technology that practically put his living room in the center of every show in ultra-definition three-D. Though he had to admit, it was the incredible video games that he appreciated most on it.

Just put it on my tab.

He clicked on the holovision, and only moments later Nathaniel was in the midst of hundreds of sheep with a not too happy shepherd trying to gather them together. He was about to sit back and change the channel when the holovision suddenly switched off.

"What the—?"

He tried the switch, but to no avail. Then, without missing a beat, the lights in the mansion turned off, leaving him in utter darkness.

"Lights on!" he commanded the 'Smart-Home' system.

No luck.

"Security!"

No response.

Nathaniel felt a slight twinge in his intestines, then got up, groping his way towards the front door. He tried to open it, but the system had bolted it shut electronically.

"Why isn't the backup power coming on?"

"Who are you talking to, Nathan?"

He froze. Did he just hear someone speak to him?

Nathaniel shook it off. Certainly he was just getting a little spooked. He would just look out the window and rap on it to get the attention of...

But there was no one outside. Not a fan. Not a photographer. Not even Masias. The streetlights were lit, and although this was a relatively busy intersection, there was not a single vehicle in sight.

"They are all gone, Nathan."

"Who said that?" he cried out, still not sure he had actually *heard* something.

"You are so alone, Nathan."

With that, Nathaniel let out an incredulous, though admittedly forced, chuckle. "Alone? Are you kidding me? I've got tens of millions of people across the planet all wanting a piece of me. I've got truckloads of fan mail arriving each day. I've got thousands of people I could call at anytime who'd do whatever I asked of them. I'm never alone! NEVER!"

"Who do you love, Nathan?"

"Love? Why I can... I..." His voice trailed off. Who the heck was he talking to anyway? This was not a voice, only some stupid thoughts in his head. He didn't need any of this; in a moment he would be surrounded by people. His fans loved him. The press loved him. He had more love than anyone else could shake a stick at.

"Who do you love?"

The tingling inside his intestines began to rise until it reached his chest; it suddenly felt as if a hundred-kilogram weight was resting on him. He began to sweat, and a disturbing sensation came over him that made him want to jump out of his skin.

"I don't need this," he whispered, trying to gain control. "I don't need you, I don't need anyone, I can do whatever I—"

And suddenly, all the lights kicked back on, accompanied by an orchestra of beeps and chirps as dozens of electronic gadgets signaled their power-up. The holovision flashed back on, and none other than *Çön Razón* was on screen, belting out one of their top hits. Nathaniel's racing heart finally began to slow.

"I'm not alone," he breathed. "I'm not alone…"

ii

Siro sat in the Oval Office opposite the embattled President Hugh Jennings Lang. He noted that the president had visibly aged over the eighteen months or so since the death of his wife and two daughters. In that short time, Lang's hair had gone from a lot of pepper with just a pinch of salt to a sparse community of pure white strands—each hair apparently desiring to quickly abandon its roots.

Still, Lang sat there before him as one maintaining the highest degree of self-assuredness, which Siro automatically attributed to an over-inflated sense of self-importance. They exchanged brief pleasantries before seating themselves— Siro on a leather couch, Lang in his chair, rolling it out from behind his massive desk. This was an incredible opportunity for Siro; it was *The Signs of the Times'* first interview with the President of the United States, and he had to admit— though only to himself—that he was a little nervous.

"Shall we begin, Mr. President?"

"By all means," Lang responded, seeming oddly eager himself. He was feeling much better these days. His cousin had been right; the music—heck, the entire experience of listening to *Çön Razón* on this musical contraption—was quite invigorating. In just over three months, he was not only back to himself again, but even feeling at the top of his game. Even the nagging irritation within him regarding the nature of the man who led this group had pretty much evaporated.

Siro noted the eager smile resting on the president's face.

He seems a bit too enthusiastic, Siro mused. *The arrogant bastard. Is he too stupid to know what I am about to do?*

Siro looked to his cameraman and nodded to begin 'rolling tape', though the truth was that he had been inconspicuously shooting the entire time, just in case there were some juicy tidbits he could edit into the piece when the president was off-guard. Though sadly, despite Siro's attempts to provide an opening for a few off-the-cuff informal comments from the president, he had had no such luck. Siro turned to the 'leader of the free world', then instantaneously transformed into his on-camera identity.

"Good morning, Mr. President. I'd first like to thank you for taking the time to meet with us. I must admit to being quite surprised that you consented to this interview."

Lang tilted his head, allowing his comfortable smile to slide into a look of pleased intrigue. "Really? Why would I miss any opportunity to speak to the American people? Granted, the office itself doesn't permit me to do these things every day—there is, of course, a flood of activity in both our nation and the world that I have to attend to from moment to moment. But I never forget who I work for."

Siro's smile slipped a little. *I'll probably need to edit that exchange out.*

"Well, certainly, Mr. President. I know that we have only an hour, so perhaps we can move forward." He looked down to his notes for a moment, then suddenly recalled the one request the president had made. Siro looked up, "Ohh, I had almost forgotten, you asked that your new deputy press secretary be present for this."

Lang nodded with a smile, as if he himself had forgotten his own request. "Oh yes, certainly, if you have no objections. I thought it would be good for him to get his feet wet."

Siro chuckled, with just a slight hint of annoyance. "Why would I object?"

Lang ignored the remark and looked off to the Secret Service agent who stood just inside the door and nodded. Siro turned to see who was entering the room when the expression on his face dropped into utter shock.

"My God…" Siro breathed as Carl Woodward walked into the room.

Woodward looked the slightest bit amused but was also clearly attempting to not appear too smug. "I thought you didn't believe in that sort of thing, Mr. Scribner."

"Brother Carl, I—"

Lang appeared intrigued, though it was unlikely he was unaware of what was transpiring. "You two know each other, I presume?"

REQUIEM

"Yes, Mr. President." It truly was difficult for Woodward to mask his pleasure. "I had a very brief stint at Mr. Scribner's news conglomerate. Quite... enlightening."

Siro's shock slowly transformed into irritation, though he was careful not to let it show. He had not seen Carl Woodward since their meeting about the...

The blood suddenly drained from Siro's face.

The list!

Siro was certain that he failed to hide his expression completely, but he struggled for only a few moments before regaining his composure. "Well, perhaps it would be best if we just started over." He would have a *lot* of editing to do on this one.

"Perhaps it would," Lang agreed.

They were down to only ten minutes left on the interview, and Siro felt he had moved past his rough start, working his way into a good rhythm by this point. He had planned to keep the initial questions relatively easy and non-combative, hoping that by the final segment, the president's guard would be let down.

Sure, a tad manipulative, but the people deserve to see him for who he is.

"So," Siro began, "let's speak on the economy a bit. No one would question that our economic growth during your tenure in office has been unprecedented. Though in reality, in the midst of all this prosperity, it seems we have become a more selfish nation. I mean, don't you think we have a responsibility to the rest of the world, which seems to be falling apart?"

Lang nodded affirmatively. "Certainly, I believe those who have been given much should give to those who have not, which is part of the reason why ten percent of our Gross Domestic Product goes to foreign aid."

"Certainly we can afford more, Mr. President. Shouldn't we spread the wealth? We are at the peak of our prosperity, and our GDP now dwarfs the rest of the world."

"This is true, Mr. Scribner, but I also never forget that this is not *my* money to be generous with. As you know, I have put our nation on an aggressive course to pay off the national debt, which was quickly nearing a hundred trillion dollars when I took office. And when it comes to helping others, you always have to ask yourself; if you give to some good cause off your credit, and you never intend to pay off that debt, is that really *you* being generous? I've dropped tax rates so that the American people, of their own free choice, can give to many good causes worldwide—I was very clear on promoting that when we dropped the rates. Still, it has to be given of their own free will."

"But you know most will just spend it on themselves."

The president shrugged his shoulders. "Perhaps, perhaps not. But I don't think it is the job of those in power—even if duly elected—to determine what to do with other people's money. I pray that their respective faiths will speak to their consciences, to do the right thing, for the right reasons."

"How can you say that when so many are suffering in the world?" Siro was quite indignant at this point.

Lang didn't miss a beat. "Your question presumes that the answer to the plight of many nations in the world is simply money. I contest that it is not. Certainly, we want to make sure that every man, woman, and child on this Earth has the basic necessities: food, clothing, shelter. But to have their governments respect their dignity as human persons, their rights, endowed by our Creator. That doesn't cost a cent, it requires a change of heart."

Siro tried to maintain just the right air of incredulity as he segued according to plan. "Let's speak to that then, Mr. President. You've brought up 'faith' a number of times during this interview. You are unabashedly a religionist. How do you justify the appropriateness of that, considering the division religious beliefs have caused not only in our nation but throughout the world?"

"Is your precious Mystic Realism so different?" Lang inquired, his eyebrow cocked.

Woodward, who had essentially blended into the furniture for the majority of the interview, struggled again not to smirk. Siro attempted a measured response.

"Why, yes, Mr. President, with all due respect, it *is* quite different. It is not a religion at all, but in many ways it is an anti-religion because it is based upon both temporal and eternal truths. We've been led to this understanding of reality by good science, psychology, sociology, anthropology, and of course philosophy. It is simply truth."

"Yet still, Mr. Scribner, with all due respect to *you*, it is still a system of beliefs; beliefs about life, ways of engaging that life, both here and in the hereafter. Whether you like the label or not, it is—by definition—a religion."

"But it's based in reality, not in myth, and it isn't burdened by ridiculous moral codes or dogmatic teachings. You don't do what is right because of fear of some invisible man in the sky punishing you if you don't. You simply harm no one, and then do as you will to do."

"Hmmm... that sounds strangely familiar."

"It should, Mr. President, because it is the truth." Siro again recomposed himself, not wanting to appear biased or defensive, though he was certainly feeling irritated at this point. He pressed on. "Have you considered that perhaps it is your being a religionist that has led to your great unpopularity, not only among the electorate, but within our legislative branch? The Congress now has a consistent veto-proof majority... *against* you."

"I'd prefer to see it as being against my *policies*."

"But you *are* your policies. Other than the Speaker of the House—who not surprisingly is a religionist himself—it seems like you don't have a friend in Congress."

Lang chuckled. "You refer to the good Speaker Abdul Ali Kareem. Yes, he is a Muslim... hardly possessing an identical belief system to the one I hold. Yet he is a man of deep humility and strong conviction. How can I find fault with that?"

But Siro was into a rhythm, firing sequential questions and not allowing that tempo to be interrupted by responding to questions returned. "Staying on topic, Mr. President, you realize Congress is looking for ways to prevent your continued divesting from American business?"

"I am attempting to get the government out of the business of running *all* business. This is for the private sector to do, for healthy competition that benefits the consumer when engaged in in an ethical manner. It's good business." Lang realized their time was running down, but at the same time he wanted to make sure that the prideful young 'journalist' felt satisfied that he was able to hit him with every zinger he desired. "But, Mr. Scribner, please do not be too anxious about this. We will maintain about ten percent ownership in most major domestic businesses because it is a good investment, not because we desire to control or even influence."

Siro, clearly frustrated at this point, was having a hard time masking his incredulity. "But don't you see, Mr. President? Your polls are lower than even President Bush's at the turn of the century. Doesn't that tell you something? People don't agree with you... they don't even *like* you!"

At this moment, Siro cut himself off. He could not believe he had let that slip out. His passion had gotten the best of him.

Still, President Hugh Jennings Lang seemed unfazed. He looked steadily at Siro. "There have been many throughout history who have foregone popularity for the sake of what was right—those who have chosen not to forsake their own private conscience for the sake of their public duties, as the good Thomas More put it. I would consider it the greatest honor to be considered in company with them."

Siro glanced down, only two minutes left.

"Understood, Mr. President. I thank you for your candor. I do have one final question."

Siro could not restrain a slight anticipatory smirk.

Here we go!

"Don't you feel you owe it to the American people to be fully transparent regarding all of your associations?"

"Certainly I do."

"Then why, Mr. President, have you not been open about your connection with organized crime—and possibly even domestic terrorism—in this country?"

Lang's congenial expression dropped, appearing more than a bit confused. He suddenly, and quite unexpectedly, found an instinct rising within himself to look over to where his musical device lay on his desk. He fought the sensation, knowing how darting eyes appeared on camera.

He's scared! Siro determined. He also felt quite pleased at the gasp from his old friend, Carl Woodward.

"I have no idea what you are talking about," Lang responded in a stern tone.

"Do you deny your close friendship with a certain Father Daniel Ananias?"

Lang's eyes narrowed, yet his anxiety began to subside. This was becoming more baffling by the moment, but he was certain that there was no legitimate attack they could level against the priest.

"I would never deny that. He is a true friend."

"A friend, really?" If Siro could have licked his chops without the camera picking up on it, now would be the time. "Did you know there are police reports that pinpoint this Roman Catholic priest's location during the Philadelphia dirty-bomb incident to right at ground zero moments before, where he was remarkably unharmed? Quite interesting I would say. And I suppose you are unaware of his close friendship and multiple continued contacts with Annie D. Nesterov, wife of the notorious Alexandre Nesterov, one-time crime boss of the Russian Syndicate?"

Lang swallowed hard; he could not mask his anger at this point, nor his revulsion over the insinuations.

Only a few more moments… then I can get back to the music…

He mustered all his strength, staring straight at Siro.

"First off, Mr. Scribner, do not underestimate the power of Divine intervention on the behalf of the faithful. Secondly, a priest ministering to a grieving parishioner should hardly be of interest or intrigue to anyone—yet truth be known, Father Daniel would invite the devil himself over for tea if he thought there was the slightest chance he could draw him closer to God!"

iii

Christopher threw the final shovel-full of dirt on the grave. He stepped back and made the Sign of the Cross as he looked out across the eleven other plots that rested on this plateau deep in the southern-most region of the Ural Mountains. Though the winter had been uncharacteristically warm to this point, a deep chill in the intermittent gusts warned that the cold would not remain at bay for long. His penitent lifestyle had seen to it that his bones and joints of sixty-one years would be home to a deepening arthritic pain.

He was near emaciated from incessant fasting, had a long and unkempt beard, and wore only a tattered cassock, underneath which he remained in a hair shirt. His days were spent in constant prayer and constant work. Christopher had been inspired to expand on the small chapel which had housed the twelve brothers for so long. Yet this expansion was beneath the chapel. Where there once were only small cells and a common dining space, over the years he had dug out an area one hundred times the size of the previous structure. Much more was to be done, but for that he would need more help.

Send your laborers, Lord, for the harvest is plenty, but the—

"Christopher."

So startled was he that the shovel flew from his hands. He spun around to see three men in black standing before him.

"We are sorry to surprise you, Holy Father."

"I no longer bear that title," Christopher responded, regathering himself. Looking more closely at the eldest of the three, he stated, "I know you." Then after a moment's thought, his eyes lit up. "You were the assistant to my predecessor, the Olivetan."

Father Tyler Ebright smiled. "Yes, it was my honor to serve the Holy Father in such a capacity at such a young age."

"As I recall, it was you that warned him against the pilgrimage to Iraq. You too were injured, were you not?"

A momentary expression of sadness traversed the face of the priest. "Yes, Holy Father, but our good Lord has seen fit to keep me around a bit longer than perhaps even I had hoped."

Christopher nodded, then turned his gaze to the youngest of the three, though still clearly middle-aged. "And you are?"

"I am Father Liam Ebright, of the Archdiocese of Philadelphia."

Then the third, probably not far from Christopher's own age, spoke up. "And I am Msgr. Craig Ebright. I serve Peter."

With that Christopher chuckled and winked. "Don't we all, Monsignor?"

Msgr. Craig smiled along with his brothers as he looked to the twelve plots. The level of disturbance of the earth upon each made it clear that all had passed in recent times. Christopher followed his gaze, reading his thoughts.

"My brothers and companions for my time of solitude and penance. One by one, each has gone on to his eternal reward in this past year. They were the companions of Brother Eli, and since his departure, they have interceded for the world with their incessant prayers. Even though all exceeded ninety years, they assisted with the work I have been called to here."

"Brother Eli?" Father Tyler inquired. "You refer to Eliot Lige?"

Christopher nodded. "Yes, this was his monastery—his fraternity—for many years. He has returned each time, along with Brother Hanoch, for the burial rite and Requiem Mass of each of his brothers. It seems they have been delayed this final time."

REQUIEM

All nodded and remained silent for a moment as an arctic wind swept through the scene. Christopher looked to the three and spoke. "So, why have you come, my brothers?"

It was Msgr. Craig who responded. "I bring you a message from His Holiness, Peter II. He states that time grows short; it is time for you to gather your flock. Those whom you disciple will be needed to care for the Remnant once the Christian Elect are no more of this Earth."

Christopher nodded solemnly. "And how does His Holiness propose I embark on such a task, now that I am alone?"

"My brothers here will remain with you and assist you. In three days, I must return to the side of Peter, for much work is at hand. But I can assure you, Your Holiness, that you will in no way be left alone."

Christopher smiled as he stroked his lengthy beard. His eyes slowly drifted until they fixed upon something behind the three brothers. "No, I do not suppose I will be."

The three priests turned to see two familiar figures standing atop a plateau nearly three hundred meters away. As they watched, from behind them emerged several dozen young men dressed in seminarian garb.

Your ways are mysterious, Lord.

5

<<n 0.233>>

NO APOLOGIES
Sister Sawlus *Defender of the Faith*

There is an old Christian saying: "How many times must I forgive my neighbor, seven times?"

I ponder this question myself as I look throughout the world and see the destruction that the so-called "followers of Christ" have caused: wars, poverty, famine, hate. And I ask myself, who are *they* to forgive?

I think of my young son and what battles he will have to fight in order to restore righteousness to the world — all because of a self-serving worn-out religion based on the fears of two men whose day will come.

As it stands now, though some fools may say otherwise, the time of the wicked Christian rule has ended. We now live in Ņeŏreƚ, the preparation for re-assumption into the Kôles.

And for those Christians who continue to preach hate and sacrilege to our children, those who refuse to see the truth, and those who insist on promoting the weakness of the body, I say this:

The time of *kathäl* arrives swiftly!

REQUIEM

i

Nathaniel twisted and turned in his bed. He was being pulled to that place again. A place from his long forgotten past, which he had attempted to keep as such.

He stood atop a castle, where hordes of infidels approached from all directions. He turned to his king, who was seated upon a mighty thrown. It was none other than Jimi T. Expo.

"Your wishes, my lord."

The Mystic King stood, his magnificent red robe cascading over his throne. His scepter glowed bright crimson. He raised it up to the sky, where bolts of lightning spewed forth from it.

"Capture them all!" he commanded.

"And what, my lord pray tell," Nathaniel continued, looking back to the masses now reaching the edge of the surrounding moat, *"shall we do with those who refuse to be captured?"*

"It is they," a different, yet strangely familiar voice chimed in, *"that shall serve as my Army of Light, to stamp out this wicked darkness which continues to consume the land."*

Nathan jerked his head back to see none other than the one called Jesse seated before him, adorned in magnificent white robes, holding a gold scepter on which a single blue stone rested.

"Y-You... Jesse?"

A gentle smile emerged from Jesse's face as the scene swept one hundred eighty degrees, and Nathaniel was now standing above Jesse, who was supine on a stretch rack. Nathaniel felt a powerful hand rest on his shoulder and a familiar voice spoke from behind him.

"Your weakness continues to show, Nathaniel. You must remember that you are one of the Chosen. I have protected you thus far, but you must come to choose your true destiny."

Nathaniel struggled for a moment, sensing the obvious disparity between the power emanating from Jimi T. and the sense of weakness that now emerged from this image of his old friend, whom he had now come to know as Jesse.

The scene changed one last time, and Nathaniel found himself lying in the center of some type of arena. The light was blinding, but he could sense that thousands of people were surrounding him. Another man was thrown down to his side, tattered and bloodied. A loud voice boomed over the jeers of the audience—the voice of the Mystic King.

"So whom then do you choose?" he called out to the crowd. *"This wretch whose name I shall not mention as it disgusts me so, or Nathaniel here?"*

The crowd roared loudly, *"NATHANIEL! WE WANT NATHANIEL!"*

Nathaniel rolled gingerly to his side, sensing pain across the surface of his own body, and met eyes with a badly beaten Jesse. Jesse whispered painfully to his old band-mate.

"The time is not yet at hand, but you can no longer remain innocent to this matter, my friend."

Jesse looked down to the back of Nathaniel's hand and witnessed the Seal. His eyes closed slowly, with a deep sense of an ageless pain. Nathaniel hastily tried to hide the mark, feeling a sudden sense of embarrassment.

"You see, Nathan," a voice called out gently from the center of the now subdued crowd, where Jimi T. had stood.

Nathan looked up with a curious sense of relief to see Jesse gracefully descending the steps towards him. Jesse walked between two lamp stands and then stood in the center of a pair of olive trees. Nathan gave a quick glance to his left, where the tattered image of Jesse had been, revealing only a pile of bones with a pair of old-style dark glasses resting amongst them.

Jesse continued, *"There are now infinite options and infinite possibilities. But in the end, it will all come down to one decision. One choice between..."*

"SEND IN THE LIONS!" the voice of Jimi T. bellowed, and in an instant a dozen lions leapt through the crowd and pounced upon Jesse, shredding him limb from limb. A reassuring hand of strength fell upon Nathaniel's shoulder as he knelt in horror before the scene.

"Call them off, Nathaniel, if you so choose..."

But he did not.

REQUIEM

ii

Pope Peter II walked slowly from the gravesite of his long-time friend, Ecumenical Patriarch Andreas II. Andreas had suffered greatly over the past year, his body covered in sores, ravaged by a disease of unknown origin. Yet the great Patriarch had embraced his suffering with joy, right to the last.

Despite the numerous funerals Peter had presided over in his more than forty years as a priest, it was the first time that he recalled celebrating one on Ash Wednesday, though appropriate he had to admit. Msgr. Craig Ebright walked alongside him towards the church.

"Just last week," the Pontiff began, "Andreas shared a dream he had with me."

"Had he foreseen his death, Holy Father?"

The Pontiff shook his head faintly. "I am not so sure. Perhaps he had, though that was not what he shared. And really, it was hard to tell what he was sharing emblematically, and what he meant literally."

Msgr. Craig, still deeply grieving the loss of the man he considered to be a second father, looked curiously towards the Pope. "What did he say, Holy Father?"

"He said that an angel had given up his wings."

Msgr. Ebright was visibly intrigued. "Surely, he must have been speaking figuratively. Did he say more?"

Pope Peter stopped walking momentarily, looking back at his assistant and friend of many years. "Only that the sacrifice this messenger of God made had left him defenseless in many ways. And if I understood Andreas correctly— and this is where I would gather the 'has given up his wings' reference applies— this angel, who has been made guardian to one very important in God's plan, is in grave danger. He has escaped the fetters of the enemy once, but a greater evil pursues him—one that could annihilate his very understanding of his own identity, his own purpose."

The monsignor pondered this thought. "I do not pretend to understand the ways of the Almighty, though it would seem that an angel who did not know his true identity or purpose could be a dangerous thing."

Peter nodded. "Yes, it would be a precarious situation, that is for certain." The Pontiff paused for another moment. "Then again, perhaps

Andreas was speaking only figuratively. There seem to be many 'lost angels' in our midst."

"This is true, Holy Father."

"Still, I must admit, it immediately struck me—the vision I had of the bound angel standing between the dragon and the American priest—could it be that there is more to this?"

"And the Holy Spirit has revealed no more to you?"

The Pontiff again shook his head as he stepped into the sacristy and began to remove his outer vestments, preparing for the trek back to his home-away-from-home. "He has not, or perhaps, through my own sinfulness and pride, I have not recognized His promptings. There is much I must take to prayer."

Again Peter paused, seemingly deep in meditation. He moved his hand briefly to his left side, the location of a somewhat painful blemish he had discovered only that morning. The blemish was peculiarly similar to the many that had covered the surface of Andreas' body. Peter sensed intuitively what this meant but did not believe it was the time to plague others with needless fear, worry, and anxiety over his health. He released the thought and immediately returned to their dialogue.

"Though this He *has* revealed to me; my exile is quickly coming to an end, before the year is up, I am sure of it. We must call our friends for one final gathering here."

With that the Pontiff pulled on an overcoat, kissed his rosary, then looked steadily at the monsignor. "What follows, I must confess, Monsignor, it will take a tremendous infusion of grace for me *not* to ask the Father to let this cup pass…"

iii

"Thank you, Brother Kako. That will be all."

The man nodded gracefully to Sister Sawlus and then saw himself out of her office. Sawlus glanced over the report Brother Kako had provided her, then pressed the button on her intercom.

"Yes, Sister Sawlus?"

REQUIEM

"Tell Brother Joran I want him in here right away," Sawlus instructed.

"Yes, Sister."

A few minutes later, Joran Waddock, director of personnel for *The Signs of the Times*, entered her office. He was an older man, in his mid-fifties, balding slightly, and perpetually nervous in the presence of the woman who had come to be known as the 'Iron Queen'.

Waddock was, in many ways, a defeated man at this point in his life. At one time holding the dignified title of *Giver of the Seal*, he had had his office rescinded (along with the Seal upon his forehead) following what most would have considered a mild indiscretion. Waddock had no doubt that Mystic Realism truly was 'The Way,' but was now also keenly aware that justice within the movement was swift, and void of any misguided sense of compassion.

"You wanted to see me, Sister?" he asked anxiously.

Sawlus released an artificial grin. "Why yes, Brother Joran. Please come in and sit down."

Waddock tried unsuccessfully to mask his slight confusion. Sister Sawlus had never spoken to him in such a congenial tone; was she finally feeling comfortable in letting her guard down with him, perhaps recognizing his inherent value to the cause? Unsure, he quickly obliged her anyway, now finding himself seated within a meter of the woman who, though perhaps half his age, invoked emotions of fear and trepidation among the masses of non-believers.

"Thank you for coming so swiftly, I do greatly admire decisiveness," Sawlus responded, still maintaining an uncharacteristically pleasant air about her. "I called you in here because there are several personnel moves which I would like you to take action on."

Waddock looked on curiously as Sawlus handed him a list with a half-dozen names on it. Waddock removed his spectacles from his coat pocket, and placing them on the bridge of his nose began reviewing the list.

As he read, Sawlus continued. "We are no longer in need of the services of those you see listed there. I would appreciate it if you handled this situation with the utmost discretion and promptness."

Waddock looked up from the list, his discomfort now fully evident, then quickly looked back down. "I-I don't understand. The people you list here have exemplary records both here and at their previous publications. I mean, Jamie Kohl is—"

"Mr. Kohl's younger brother is currently a seminarian in the Roman

Catholic Archdiocese of Philadelphia. A bit too close to home, wouldn't you say, Brother Joran?"

Waddock looked up to Sister Sawlus, an expression of shock on his face. "Having a brother who is a seminarian is not a cri—"

"Don't tell me what is and is not a crime, you old fool!" chided Sawlus, her more familiar nature now emerging. "The rules of man written on paper do not change the spiritual laws of existence!"

Waddock was taken aback by the forcefulness of Sawlus' conviction, and the rapid dissipation of her previous congenial disposition. He found himself looking absently back at the sheet of paper in his hands. He spoke tentatively.

"And Terrence Aborn?"

"The waffling fool. His eldest son is a Christian involved in the so-called 'pro-life' movement."

Waddock was now fully in dismay, but he could not find it within himself to stop this apparent madness.

"And Jenny Carlin?"

"She's been seen spending a great deal of time with a male who has been identified as a writer and editor for the largest underground Christian magazine in the nation. Very dangerous."

Waddock looked down, closed his eyes, and slid his thumb and forefinger under his spectacles, pressing against what he sensed was an oncoming tension headache. His interior struggle did not escape the 'Iron Queen'.

"It's apparent that you are not in support of my decisions. Either that, or perhaps you don't recognize my authority to do so."

Waddock leaned back, running his hand though what remained of his hair. He realized he was sweating, but he would have to maintain his composure—perhaps even for his own safety. Weakness did not ingratiate one to the woman who sat before him. "No, Sister, it's not that. It's just that there are still laws against firing a person based on religion or associations."

Sawlus smiled condescendingly. "Don't be so spineless—and so lacking in creativity, Brother Joran. I don't care *what* you give them as the reason for their release. I just want you to see to it that it happens. Don't you see it, Brother? There is a disease among us. It's called *Christianity*. It is the scourge of humankind's existence and could spell the doom for us all. Do you know anything about history? Have you ever heard of the Inquisition? The Crusades? The Salem witch trials? Surely you've at least heard of the Holocaust?"

Waddock nodded solemnly. He had heard this litany used before. "I have."

"Then can you possibly be so blind? We are allowing *carriers* in our midst, and we must be strong enough to take a stand."

Not using his best judgment, which he would later regret, Waddock again stumbled in, "But Aborn's got a wife who suffers from ALS, and three children still at home. He worked seven years with the Walnut Community Organization, and then three at *Global Times* before we bought them out. He can—"

"Perhaps," Sawlus interrupted, "he should have thought about all that a while back and gotten his family in order so it would never have had to come to this."

Waddock was dumbfounded and could no longer think of anything to say.

Sawlus continued, "I want this to be taken care of by the end of the day. Do I make myself clear?"

Waddock, realizing the uselessness of fighting, nodded slowly.

"Thank you, Brother Joran. Well I guess you have your workday cut out for you."

Waddock nodded again, stood up, and solemnly exited the room. Sister Sawlus sat back in her chair, pondering an apparently weighty issue for a moment. She nodded to herself and reached for the intercom button.

"Yes, Sister?" the voice came across.

"Yes, Reba, please write an *e*memo from me to Brother Joran Waddock, dated tomorrow, stating that effective immediately, he has been terminated from this company. Please cite insubordination as the basis for his release."

"Yes, Sister, understood. Also, there is a call waiting for you. He says he is a priest, the last name's Ebright…"

Sawlus' eyes momentarily widened, then quickly narrowed. *Which one?*

But she did not miss a beat. "You tell that pathetic deceiver of souls that I would sooner consume broken glass than speak to him!" Then an obviously pleasing thought struck her. "And while you are at it, put Brother Kako on his trail. Dig up something good, and I'll put it on the front page next week."

6

And then the *Neōret* [1] will begin, and all days that have gone before will be no more. The 360-day cycle of the *Kōles* will again be impressed upon the €arth, and the 5-day celebration of *Kat'hāl* [2] will once more be instituted throughout the land.

Habor T: 5-8
Book of Given Truths

[1] Translation approximation; "New Beginning of the End"
[2] Literally; "Purging"

i

Nathaniel inhaled deeply, holding the smoke in for as long as he could, then released it slowly. He closed his eyes and smiled, daintily handing Siro the joint as if it were some magical elixir. This had been the first chance at a true break since the completion of *Çön Razón's* nine-month world tour.

Siro smiled dreamily himself, looking back at Nathaniel. "This stuff is awesome. I haven't smoked weed since I was a kid! I... I truly cherish these moments."

Siro took a deep hit himself, and Nathaniel found himself suddenly struck with an odd compulsion to giggle.

Siro was unable to hold the hit in and coughed deeply. "What, man? What's so funny?"

Nathaniel burst into a fit of laughter, which quickly turned into a series of coughs. Upon recapturing his breath, he was finally able to choke out, "Sorry, Siro, couldn't help myself."

Siro's amusement transformed quickly into annoyance. "Well, I like the stuff, but you know it'd be better doing some *Cimä*."

Nathaniel shook his head. "No thanks, bud. This does me fine."

Siro stood from the middle of his living-room floor, took a few unsteady steps, then collapsed on his couch. He rolled over on his back, then looked back at his friend.

"So how's the rock 'n roll lifestyle treating you?" he asked.

Nathaniel shrugged, looking neither pleased with nor interested in the question.

Despite the haziness of his current condition, Siro recognized his friend's look of displeasure.

"What gives, Nathaniel?"

Nathaniel shook his head. "Man, I don't know. I mean, it's awesome, don't get me wrong, but the truth is, sometimes I don't feel like I'm in a band at all. I mean, I don't know the guys—at least anything about them—and they clearly have no interest in getting to know me. And Jimi T.'s never anywhere to be seen or heard."

Siro provided an expression of understanding. "Yeah, Jimi T. is definitely someone who enjoys his privacy. And you've got to remember, he's a busy—"

"Yeah, man," Nathaniel cut in, loathing the thought of hearing the 'busy man' motif one more time. "But it's not... it's not like a tight band. We don't sit down and write together like me and J— " He caught himself. "Like my old band used to. Sometimes I wonder why Jimi T. even brought me into this project."

Siro shrugged. "Well, a lot of people wondered that at first, but after hearing you, no one questions it anymore."

There was a long pause, as both appeared to be deep in thought. Finally, Nathaniel, looking for a brighter subject, spoke up.

"So when do I get to meet your *Þreha*, the *Iron Maiden*?"

"Screw you!" Siro fired back, subsequently grabbing his shoe from the floor and flinging it at Nathaniel.

The tension broke instantly, despite the fact that the shoe hit Nathaniel squarely in his chest, and the room was filled with high-pitched laughter. After the hysterics diminished some, Siro spoke again.

REQUIEM

"I don't know. Why don't you invite us over to your L.A. mansion sometime for dinner? Then you can call her 'Iron Queen' to her face. But I suggest you wear a pair of armored jockey shorts!"

Nathaniel nodded, finding himself giggling again. "Cool, I've been looking for an excuse to throw a party. I'll buzz you two as soon as I get it together. I can only handle this mystery of the 'Iron Queen's' identity for so long."

ii

Sister Sawlus walked anxiously down the hallway with her son, Caleb. She had only met the Mystic King one time before and felt completely overwhelmed by the occasion. Still, she was thrilled that he had asked her to meet with him, and had even asked her to bring her son along, who was, without a doubt, the Mystic King's number one fan.

Sawlus walked hand-in-hand with Caleb into the reception area, and before the receptionist could even look up, Jimi T. called out from his office.

"Please come in, Sister. I have been waiting."

Sawlus felt a twinge of anxiety sweep through her upon hearing the deep voice seasoned with just a touch of English accent, but she quickly purged the sensation from her being. She tightened her grip on Caleb's hand and walked calmly into the office.

Sawlus laid eyes on the now infamous Jimi T. Expo, who was casually leaning back in his chair, wearing blue jeans, a black T-shirt, and what looked like some sort of riding boots. His glasses were as dark as ever, and his characteristic hint of a smile did not disappoint. Her eyes were then caught, momentarily, by the figure standing in the far left corner of the office.

Tæsír Hoc provided Sawlus with a carefully measured grin. A feeling of revulsion swept through her, and she immediately noticed the expression on both The Prophet and Jimi T.'s faces change momentarily. Sawlus quickly recomposed herself and looked towards Jimi T.

"My lord," she stated respectfully, bowing her head.

A more deliberate smile emerged from the Mystic King's face, but then his attention was caught by the eyes of Caleb. A look of pleasant curiosity emerged from Jimi T.'s countenance as he motioned for the boy to approach.

Without so much as a moment's hesitation, Caleb released his mother's hand and walked over to the Mystic King. Uncomfortably, Sawlus attempted to introduce the pair, "This is my s—"

But Jimi T. raised his hand, commanding her silence, as he stepped forward from his chair. He smoothly dropped to one knee and knelt face-to-face with Caleb.

"What is your name, young child?"

Caleb stopped less than a meter in front of the Mystic King and stated without hesitation, "I-I am C-Caleb."

Jimi T. looked curiously at him. "Caleb, son of who?"

Sawlus again tried to intervene but was cut off with only a slight, yet deliberate, adjustment of Jimi T.'s head.

"I-I do not kn-kn-know m-my f-father."

Jimi T. looked up to Sawlus as he stood. "Certainly, the boy must have a father."

"Yes," Sawlus began anxiously, her eyes darting towards Tæsír Hoc for only a second. "It's just that...that..."

Jimi T. sensed the discomfort of the subject and held his hand up once again, motioning her to stop. "Perhaps another time, Sister. I'm sure you have your reasons."

He stood and looked down again at Caleb, who tilted his head backwards to smile back up at his Mystic King.

"How long before he reaches the Age of Ascension?" Jimi T. inquired, now looking to Tæsír Hoc.

"About five months, my lord. I have already made arrangements for—"

"I will perform the *Ko'nąsarñiä*," Jimi T. cut in, though in such a serene fashion, it was barely noted as an interruption.

Tæsír Hoc appeared taken aback, and after looking briefly at Sister Sawlus, spoke out, "My lord, it's already been—"

"I said," Jimi T. responded, with the slightest hint of anger in his voice, "that I will perform the ceremony."

There was a moment of uncomfortable silence in the room, and then Sawlus stepped forward. "My lord, I would be honored if you would perform the *Ko'nąsarñiä* for my son."

REQUIEM

The slight trace of a smile returned to Jimi T.'s face as he continued to gaze down at Caleb. He grasped the boy by both shoulders. "And on that day, Caleb, you will be given a new father."

"Th-th-th-thanks, m-my lord."

Jimi T. released the boy, then casually moved back behind his desk, sitting down. With his gaze still lowered, he addressed Tæsír Hoc.

"I want you to make the arrangements immediately."

"But with all due respect, my lord, it is my respons—"

Jimi T. raised his head towards the Prophet, who now realized he had overstepped his bounds, and would be entering dangerous territory if he went any further.

"That is twice you have questioned me in front of a Member of The Way. Do not let there be a third time."

"Yes, my lord," Tæsír Hoc responded in a manner which neared sulking. Sawlus could not help but feel a mild sense of amusement watching the Great Prophet being put in his place.

"In any case," Jimi T. continued, looking up to Sawlus and motioning for her to sit in the chair in front of him, "this is not what I actually called you in for."

Sawlus sat as instructed and looked at Jimi T. attentively as he leaned back and pulled one leg up on his armrest. He pondered a thought briefly, then gave voice to it. "Sister Sawlus, I have a great deal of respect for you and your work. I feel you are a true asset to The Way."

Sawlus smiled bashfully, "Why thank you, my lord."

"Still," Jimi T. continued as if she had not even spoken. "I do ask some changes from you."

Sawlus was puzzled. "My lord?"

"I need you to temper this anti-Christian campaign you've initiated."

Sawlus appeared shocked. "But, my lord! They are the scourge! It even states it in *The Book of Given Truths*, and the *Book of Hoc* further elaborates on how Christianity has nearly spelled the death of us all on many occasions!"

Tæsír Hoc smiled in his own self-gratifying way, but quickly rescinded when he realized that this would not be the best expression for the Mystic King to see, all things being considered.

Jimi T. smiled himself in a conciliatory fashion. "Your passion in your beliefs is inspiring. The *Kôles* flows freely through you. Yet nonetheless, you are in jeopardy of cutting off a large portion of the *Kôles* which might otherwise be salvaged."

Sawlus was dumbfounded. "My lord?"

"You must understand, Sister, that the Christians of today do not know any better than what they have been taught. They have been gravely misled through no fault of their own. To hold something against them which they could not possibly control would be prejudiced in the extreme, and that I cannot tolerate."

Sawlus bit her lip, feeling both confused and embarrassed, as Jimi T. continued.

"It is our responsibility to help the Christians understand where they, as a people, have fallen astray, so that we may lead them back to the true light— the *Kôles*. They are nothing more than sheep led astray by a deceptive shepherd. A strong, yet caring hand could lead them back into the fold. Do you not understand?"

As much as she wished to fight it, there was more than just a hint of logic to what the Mystic King was saying. Sawlus was also fully aware that this was not a discussion or a debate, yet an order to be obeyed to the letter.

"I will do as you say, my lord."

"Very well," Jimi T. responded. "We shall allow all of the non-enlightened a grace period—an opportunity to learn the truth. When that period has concluded, then we shall explore other measures."

Jimi T. rose from his seat, quickly followed by Sawlus. Tæsír Hoc stepped forward from his previous place of standing.

"I can see Sister Sawlus out, my lord, if it pleases you."

Jimi T. looked briefly at the Prophet, provided a light shrug, and then looking at Sawlus, extended his arm toward the door. "Your presence has been most... appreciated."

Caleb, realizing it was time to leave, scrambled out ahead of them.

Once out in the hall, Caleb skipped up and down, seemingly intrigued by whatever was written on any message boards aligning both sides of the corridor.

Tæsír Hoc took Sister Sawlus by the arm and whispered into her ear,

"Do not worry about what he says about taking such a hard line with the Christians. You are doing the right thing—he just has to take that softer approach for... for political reasons."

"Oh?" responded Sawlus, seemingly disinterested as she pulled her arm away and continued to follow her son down the hall.

The Prophet looked up to Caleb, who was now jumping from side to side down the steps, switching hands on the handrail as he cheered himself.

"So," he continued, "you have still decided to keep his father's identity from him. *Tsk Tsk!* I am surprised at you, Sister."

Sawlus looked at the Tæsír with an expression of disgust on her face. "When *I* decide it's time he should know, then *I* will tell him!"

"The truth?"

"Of course the truth!"

The Prophet grinned, seemingly enjoying the tension he was able to generate in this woman who intrigued him so. He grasped her hand. "Well then, *Sister*, what say you and I go back to my temple for true joining? I have greatly missed—"

Sawlus yanked her hand away from him and looked him straight in the eye. "I've told you that it's over! It's been over for almost two years you stupid prick! Can't you get that through your thick damned skull?"

His eyes narrowed. "Dear me, so *passionate*, Sister. Your language is quite... *delicious* I would say." Then, transitioning into a more aggravated tone, he said, "It's that Siro pipsqueak, isn't it?"

"Who I choose as my *Ðreða* is no concern of yours!"

"And having a *Ðreða* in no way excludes you from intimate relations with another member of The Way. In fact, it is strongly encouraged in—"

"Yes I know, in the *Book of Hoc!* But I want to make something clear to you; I am no longer interested in you. I feel nothing but disgust when I look at you. Good day... or bad... I don't give a shit!"

With that Sawlus hastened towards the door at the end of the hallway, where Caleb now stood.

"You know," the Prophet called out from behind her in a lightly sinister tone, "the boy really has the right to know of his father..."

DOMINION

iii

Phineas knelt before the Blessed Sacrament in the small inner-city chapel, given the name of St. Maximilian Kolbe, and up until now, entrusted to the care of Father Daniel Ananias. In fact, it had been the structure in which Fr. Daniel had prayed, and been miraculously protected, when the dirty bomb had gone off not more than twenty meters away.

His mentor had received confirmation that he would be transferred to a location in upstate New York, in a small town called Pittsford, close to where the mass-suicide sect had been located. No real explanation had been given, but Father Daniel trusted in God's providence. If the Cardinal-Archbishop requested it, as far as Father Daniel was concerned, Jesus Christ Himself desired this of him.

Phineas had found this chapel to be of great consolation to him. It was a place where he could further work through, with the help of the Spirit, his complex and troubled past. Though he believed fully in the Sacrament of Reconciliation, and that his sins were truly forgiven, he felt that he still bore the scars of a past life lived far from God. His emotional and psychological healing was still in progress.

"For sure, *Bon Dieu*," he whispered. "A slow cure is a sure cure."

Images of the many 'ceremonies' his Haitian-Creole mother would have him participate in as a child began to fill his head. Phineas had learned to trust that whatever the Lord had sought to put before him while immersed in prayer, he would go with, offering the scene up to the Lord, and requesting a healing of the memory. Ultimately, he would seek the truth, and even redemption of the matter.

The different items and artifacts utilized within the practice of Santería—his mother's ancient religious system brought over from Haiti—had once intrigued the curious boy, but now felt stale, even unsettling. How many times had she 'prayed' over him? How many 'spells' were cast? The images swirled in Phineas' mind, then suddenly, they dissipated, and he was no longer reminiscing in the past. A vivid image of his mother in the present came before him.

"Phinny, my boy, to who you've been talkin'?"

Anxiety gripped Phinny, as he was unsure whether this apparition was truly his mother or only his mind playing tricks on him, drawing on old misguided feelings and past guilt.

"Don't be defyin' me, boy. You are my seed. You'll not be escapin' dat!"

His heart began to race. This seemed far too real.

"You want to be fightin' me, boy? I'll not have it! I still have a piece of you, and I'll not be lettin' go."

At this point in his vision, Phinny saw his mother reach out to his chest, but she suddenly stopped, a look of irritation on her face. She then reached up to his forehead, her hand passing straight through his skull as she smiled, then she pulled back her hands into a cupped position.

She looked down, gazing upon what she had cupped in her hands as if holding a baby chick, then she looked back to her son, her smile transforming into more of a sneer.

"You'll not be gettin' away dat easy, boy."

And with that, she opened her hands, and to Phinny's dismay, he saw a chunk of brain tissue pulsating as if it possessed its own life. Though it was clear that the tissue was not healthy; there were black tumors, like a cancer, all over and within it. The cancerous tissue was so intertwined with the healthy that it could not be clearly discerned.

"You tink dem gifts come from dat god of yours? Dey is not! Dey is from me, boy…"

Despite his momentary terror, Phinny would not heed.

"Passe', Satan," he breathed.

The vision collapsed upon itself, and as it drew away, Phinny watched the countenance of his mother distort into something much more grotesque before vanishing completely.

7

"Music gives a soul to the universe, wings to the mind,
flight to the imagination, and life to everything."

– Plato

i

Annie D. Nesterov wept as Father Daniel poured another cup of tea.

"Annie, you must let this go and trust in the merciful hand of God.
Your sins have been forgiven. You need not torment yourself so."

"Aye, Father. I may be forgiven, but I won't be forgettin'. A horrible
thing I've done, and my Alex will be payin' for it eternally."

Father Daniel filled his own cup, then sat down across the table. With
his relocation imminent, and Annie D.'s continued fragile state, he was
considering inviting her to come with him and Phineas, perhaps even serving as
a maternal presence for the boy.

"He made his own decisions, Annie. You could not control that."

"I drove him to it, Father! I refused to forgive him! Blessed are the
merciful for mercy will be theirs—that's what the Good Book says. I'll be
judged with the same judgment I passed meself!"

"Is it your salvation that you fear?"

"Always, Father. But in this case, it's for Alex. I've prayed for him, and
me children of course, incessantly. Four rosaries a day, a Chaplet of the Divine
Mercy each hour. The Mass, the Angelus…"

She trailed off, and again began to weep.

Always being comfortable with silence among friends, Father Daniel
waited for the tortured soul before him to speak again without his prompting.

"Is it too late, Father?" she managed to get out between tears. "Is it too late for any of them?"

Father Daniel shook his head. "No, Annie. God hears your prayers, and prayers are directed into eternity, so your requests now are not without efficacy, and your suffering not without merit."

Annie D. nodded, a small trace of a pained smile emerging even as she looked down again. It had been hard for her, trying to find even a spark of hope in a life where she had buried not only her husband but all of her children and children's children.

Did they call upon you, Lord, at that moment of separation from this life? Did they accept Your offerin' of mercy, even if they hadn't reflected it completely in their lives? They're still your children, Lord…

"…have mercy on their souls!"

Annie did not realize her thoughts had become manifest in words.

"Annie?"

"Aye," she spoke now, barely above a whisper. "Forgive me, Father. I must know. What more can I do?"

Father Daniel gazed at Annie evenly. "Annie, I do not necessarily want to dissuade you from your incessant prayers of intercession. But you must remember; it is not the frequency or even the words, but the disposition of the heart that matters. A one-phrase prayer of supplication offered in earnest humility will have greater efficacy than a hundred rosaries spoken in rote, when the heart is pure and fully disposed to the will of God."

Annie D. eyed her pastor intently. "Are you sayin', Father, that I should stop?"

"By no means, Annie! Storm heaven with your prayers! I only caution you; do so with the trust of a child in her loving daddy, her 'Abba'. It is He who desires their salvation more than even you."

ii

"So you're leavin' us, yo?"

The young inner-city teen was none too pleased at the words Phineas had spoken. He, along with several dozen others of his own ilk, had been coming to a youth group facilitated by 'Deacon P.' for seven months now. Yet, as they stood on the sidewalk in front of the St. Maximilian Kolbe Blessed Sacrament Chapel, there was a clear sense of disappointment—bordering upon resentment—among the crew.

"*Tanpri*, Jerome. It isn't permanent. Really, nothing is permanent here. We have to each find the path the Lord has laid before us."

"But who's gonna put up with us, yo? Ain't Nobody else ever made sense of this Jesus stuff."

Phineas nodded. He had asked himself the same question, though he did not want his youth group to pick up on his own hesitancy.

"I trust in God, Jerome. If He has called me to another place, then He has a plan for you all as well."

"He gonna let us in on this plan, yo?"

Phineas was about to respond when his eyes were suddenly caught by something across the street. A young woman wearing dark sunglasses and a boy emerged from *The Signs of the Times* building. It was clear she did not wish to be noticed, as she looked down and hurried to a vehicle parked at the end of the block.

The young boy, perhaps no more than five, was scanning the entire scene. As he turned his gaze towards Phineas and the crowd of boys, Phineas suddenly dropped to his knees, now shielded from the sight of the boy by the members of the youth group.

"Deacon P., what are you—?"

"We must pray! Now! Pray that *Le Bon Dieu* provides for us all in these times of uncertainty!"

The group was confused at the suddenness of it all but obliged their mentor. Phineas kept his head bowed but was able to see the boy enter the vehicle out of the corner of his eye. A moment later, the car pulled off, but Phineas could sense—sense clearly—the eyes of the youngster gazing at the unusual scene of a group of hoodlums praying on the sidewalk. Still, Phineas felt fairly confident that the boy had not seen him.

"*Felipe.*"

"What?" Phineas responded to the utterance.

Jerome looked up. "Deacon P.? You losin' it, bro?"

Phineas looked about him and suddenly realized that the word had not been audibly spoken. He looked about the group he had mentored these months. Not one of them bore that name.

"Does anyone here know someone by the name of Felipe?"

"Yeah, there's a Filipino boy in the block called that."

Something inside of Phineas leapt at this point. It was not a movement of emotion, but of the Spirit. He was sure of it.

"You must bring me to him. I believe he is the one that will lead you once I have gone."

At that statement, the entire group broke out spontaneously in laughter, though it quickly subsided when it was clear that their mentor did not share the joke.

"*Sa ena?* What is it?" Phineas inquired, not used to being a source of amusement to others.

"Yeah, ahh, Deacon P., you got the wrong guy—most def—yo. First off, the boy's only seven. We were all at his First Communion last week. Second, he's retarded. The boy don't speak no sense."

There were some chuckles and snickers among the crowd, but that again quickly dissipated.

And a child shall lead them. Phineas mused, not certain the thought was his own. *Your ways are mysterious, Lord.*

"Bring me to him."

iii

"That was incredible!" exclaimed Siro as he burst into his house, one arm draped around Sister Sawlus, the other reaching for the wall in an attempt to balance himself.

"*That* it was," Sawlus responded, as she helped the more-intoxicated Siro into his bedroom. It had been a somewhat anxious evening for her. Though she and Siro had engaged in many group-joining sessions, this was the first time that someone whom she had 'joined' with in the past without Siro's knowledge had participated.

Although Sawlus was by no means morally bound from engaging in 'the joining' with others as she chose, she and Siro had an unspoken agreement that they would only see each other. And though she did not necessarily feel this agreement inhibited her from acting on her desires at a moment's notice, she would generally prefer not have to deal with the unavoidable whining that would accompany Siro's discovery of her activities.

In the end it was not a problem, as her former liaison did not even seem to remember her. This small blow to Sawlus' ego was a meager price to pay for the potential aggravation it saved her.

Sawlus dropped Siro onto his bed. He immediately sat up and motioned for her to join him.

She smiled coyly. "Not just yet, big boy. I need a drink."

She walked out of the room and made her way to the kitchen to fix herself a nightcap. As she approached the kitchen, Sawlus noticed that the light on the holophone was blinking. She turned to call up to Siro, then decided he was probably out cold by now anyway. She stepped up to the machine, her curiosity never an impulse to be curbed, and pushed the 'play' button.

Sawlus jerked uncomfortably as the image of a man flashed before her. She had never quite gotten used to these contraptions, but that was still not the reason for her to feel as startled as she did today.

The figure smiled widely and spoke.

"Hey, bro! It's your favorite rock 'n roll star! Just dropping you a line as promised. I'm going to have that party I told you about next Thursday at sundown. I'm counting on you and the 'Iron Maiden' to be there. Oops! Guess I'm in deep crap, huh? Anyway, I'd love to finally get to meet her, and it's always grand seeing you. Rock 'n roll, buddy!"

Before she could make a move, a second message flashed on, and she felt an instant wave of revulsion as she saw the Prophet before her.

"Brother Siro, it would be good for us to meet in the immediate. There are some things regarding your precious little *Þreħa* that I feel the need to inform you of. I will be in your city within the week. Contact me straightaway."

The figure flashed off, and Sawlus took a few deep breaths as her pulse slowed. As strong as she appeared to the masses, there were still some ghosts from her past she was not yet ready to face.

The machine responded, "Press the erase button to delete the most recent message. Press and hold to delete all messages."

Sawlus stepped cautiously back up to the machine, took an uncertain look back at Siro's bedroom, reached down, and pressed the button.

8

"We see things not as they are but as we are."

– John Milton

i

Father Daniel stood at the one end of the table, an assisting seminarian to either side of him. Phineas Savoie lay supine, continuing to convulse.

The priest did his best to prevent the boy from banging his head, while the two seminarians each held an arm.

Phineas' seizures had occurred intermittently since his childhood, but it was only in the past few weeks that they took on a different, quite intriguing character. He was now at the point that they were occurring every three to four days, yet their more violent stage would last only a few moments.

As anticipated, the convulsions stopped, and Phineas breathed deeply. The seminarians exchanged uncomfortable glances as Father Daniel motioned them to step away.

"We must give him room now. He will speak."

It really was a mixed blessing. As traumatic as the event would be for him, once the convulsions ended, Phineas would provide information regarding the activities of the darker movement, especially those close to the 'Iron Queen', Sister Sawlus. These moments of supernatural insight had provided the Christian underground movement with critical information, allowing them to stay just one step ahead of their relentless foe.

At that moment, Phineas sat up, retaining a glazed look in his eyes. Father Daniel, after a moment, stepped forward.

"Who am I speaking to?" the priest inquired.

Phineas turned to Father Daniel with a perplexed, somewhat anxious, expression on his face. He opened his mouth, and spoke.

"I-I-I am th-the ch-ch-child."

ii

Caleb bolted upright in his bed, feeling that not only his breath, but his very *soul* had snuck back into his body by way of his nostrils just a moment before he had awakened.

His mind had drifted away again. Perhaps feeling as if it had been *pulled* away was a more accurate description of the sensation. Despite his curious nature, Caleb knew that being forced to do anything was against the wishes of the Spiritual Entity, and a concept not of the *Kôles*. But each time, though somewhat reluctant, he had agreed to the game.

He always returned from these experiences with almost no information, however, save a memory of a 'dark man'. Though his skin was brown, the young man, perhaps even a boy, had glowing emerald-green eyes.

In the dream, Caleb knew that the man told him his name. Still, upon his return to his own room, he could not remember a word that had been spoken. The dark man would simply step forward, grasp hold of him, and anything beyond that was not retained in Caleb's memory.

Caleb shuddered. He felt a mixed sensation of shame, curiosity, and confusion churning within him. He pondered the thought of going into his mother's room to tell her what had happened but then decided against it. Mother had brought home several men that night and was participating in the 'joining' with them in her bedroom.

He was strictly forbidden to interrupt his mother during this most sacred ceremony. He had learned his lesson after being brutally chastised by his mother after her shrieks had become too loud for him to bear and he had ran into her room. That was when Caleb learned that clothing was not a requirement for the 'joining'.

He only heard a few random thumps from the next room and decided that his fears could be bottled up and tucked away for the time being. He lay back down in his bed, pulled the covers over his head, and prayed to the Spiritual Entity to protect him through the night.

REQUIEM

iii

Nathaniel walked off the stage, following another soul-moving performance by *Çön Razón*. This particular performance had been a benefit concert to raise money for women's health services throughout the third world.

"We must care for our mothers," Jimi T. had said. "For it is the Mother of us all that cares for us."

As was always the case following a performance, Nathaniel was feeling a bit dreamy. He stepped backstage, bypassing the personal dressing rooms of his other band-mates, finally coming upon his own. He placed his hand upon the palm recognition device and pulled it back suddenly as it gave him a mild shock.

"What the—?"

The door suddenly opened, and a gush of air burst through. After shielding his eyes and face momentarily, Nathan peered through the portal. But instead of seeing his couch and other amenities, what he saw was a clearing in the midst of a sparse forest. Not too far off, he could see a fairly good-sized tree with a young boy sitting at its base. The boy looked up curiously at Nathan.

Nathan, feeling somewhat intrigued himself, stepped through the portal and into the scene. He walked towards the boy, whom he now realized was humming. The tune was strangely familiar, though Nathan could not quite place it. He then noticed another sound—something like wind chimes—though the sounds were not random, as one would expect. The chimes seemed to mimic the tune the boy was humming—or was it the other way around?

As Nathan got within ten meters of the boy, he hesitated upon seeing the gravestones before him. Most of the names were familiar. He saw the name 'Jesse Chardin', which he somehow surmised was the real name of his one-time friend, then known as Jonathan Storm. Though it was more the one next to it that caught his eye. It read 'Tobias Isaac Chardin', and it gave off the subtlest crimson-red hue.

"I did not expect this visit," the boy stated, having ceased his tune.

Nathan looked curiously at him. He was no more than six or seven years of age and dark-haired. Nathan also noticed, not a meter away from the boy, a set of crushed sunglasses.

"Do I know you?"

The boy smiled gently, though his eyes maintained an expression of intense curiosity. *"In this particular manifestation, perhaps not, yet you are close to me, Nathan. Even more so, you are close with my brother, perhaps closer than would be desired."*

Nathan was perplexed. The boy began to hum again, and the delicate sound of the wind chimes returned. Nathan looked up to the tree upon which the boy rested. It seemed strong and healthy, though it also invoked a sense of *sadness*, even *regret* within him.

"It is a symbol," the boy said, having completed his song and noted Nathan's gaze.

"A symbol of what?"

"Of a promise made many years ago—a promise believed to have been in vain. The seed has been planted, though the soil has been tainted."

"I do not understand," Nathan countered.

"Then do not close off your heart, Nathan. You have encountered the Fruit of Humanity… though its state is unclear. All is not as it should be, but a response will be required."

"A response?"

And with that, another tune became manifest. This one, however, did not carry the beautiful mellifluous melody as the chimes had provided. Instead, a loud cacophony sounded out which seemed as if an infinite number of stringed instruments were striking dissonant sounds at the same time. Nathan was about to cover his ears when he sensed a transformation—not in the music, but within his own ears. He began to discern something with less of a discord, something not necessarily pleasing, but clearly *seductive*.

"Do not be deceived, my friend."

"What?"

And as the scene began to fade, Nathan noted a spot of blood appearing on the boy's chest, slowly growing, until all went black.

iv

Tæsír Hoc, visibly flustered, entered the office of Jimi T. Expo.

"Your timing is, to say the least, a bit inconvenient," the Prophet asserted to the back of the chair upon which the Mystic King was seated. "I have been making preparations for the Black Festival."

Jimi T. turned his chair from behind his desk so that he was now facing Tæsír Hoc.

"I am aware of your preparations. That is precisely why I have called you here."

The Prophet's expression changed as he allowed an anticipatory smile to emerge from his face. "You have some inspirations you wish to add to the celebration?"

"I do."

Tæsír Hoc looked on anxiously at Jimi T. Perhaps he had misjudged his superior's dismissive nature to just about all he had done within The Way. Yet, the Mystic King just looked back, or at least *seemed* to look back at him from behind those dark glasses. The silence became uncomfortable, and the Prophet spoke out again.

"Forgive me, my lord, but what do you wish us to do for the celebration?"

"Nothing."

Tæsír Hoc hesitated momentarily, having been caught off-guard by this response.

"Again, forgive me, my lord, you want us to do—?"

"Nothing, and do not ask me to repeat it again, if you please."

The Prophet felt fire begin to well up within him. "I do not understand. This is the first Black Festival of the *Neöret*. The people have been waiting all year to celebrate *Kat'häl*. It is their opportunity to release their primal feelings and—"

He ceased speaking as the Mystic King rose from his seat and leaned forward across the desk. Tæsír Hoc's eyes widened as a reddish glow seemed to emanate from behind Jimi T.'s dark shades. Still, not even a hint of tension could be read on his face.

"I will not say it again. The Black Festival of *Kat'häl* is violent, destructive, and—"

"And it is beautiful!" the Prophet interjected, allowing his passion to get the best of him.

DOMINION

I will not allow this! You have gone too far!

"Have I?"

Tæsír Hoc immediately realized his mistake and quickly looked away. The reddish glow in the Jimi T.'s eyes grew momentarily, then faded.

The Mystic King paused, allowing the breath of the moment to pass. "Yes, it *is* beautiful, but an outward display of this festival will destroy everything that we have built here thus far. The masses are not yet ready for five days of unbridled anarchy from our people. They will turn against our movement, and all could be lost."

Tæsír Hoc struggled to assume dominion over the conflicting feelings inside of him. He resisted the instinct to call out angrily at the cowardice of this man—the so-called *Anointed One*. The interior maelstrom was pushing the Prophet to the point a point he feared he could not return from. He managed only to look down and mumble through gritted teeth.

"Then how are our people to celebrate *Kat'häl*?"

The Mystic King stood upright, then again seated himself in his chair. A slight trace of a smile emerged from his face. It seemed that the more the Great Prophet became enraged, the more this man grew in serenity. He spoke now with a more soothing tone, which his subordinate could only interpret as condescension.

"They may celebrate it in their hearts..."

9

i

Several hundred people, consisting of political, religious, and community leaders—along with a few stray reporters—waited anxiously outside the Philadelphia mansion of Jimi T. Expo. It was the eve of the completion of the first cycle of *Neöret,* and the Mystic King was about to make an announcement reportedly every bit as earth shattering as the message he had conveyed a year ago today.

The front door opened, and the now familiar procession emerged. First, Brother Siro Scribner, followed by Brother Esau LaVey, then Tæsír Hoc, then the Mystic King himself. A fifth man emerged with the procession today, whom all in the audience quickly recognized as presidential candidate William Maison, President Pro Tempore of the U.S. Senate, and the highest-ranking political figure involved with The Way of Mystic Realism. Several other men, obviously some form of security, flanked the crew.

Jimi T. stepped up to the podium as the others fell in behind him, resembling, to some degree, a high-profile police line-up.

"The Spirit be with you," he greeted.

DOMINION

Reflexively, the crowd returned the Mystic King's greeting.

"I am here today to announce the next step in implementing the will of the *Kôles*." He paused momentarily, taking a moment to deliberately look out across his audience. "As you know, I am greatly troubled by the state of affairs in our world today, and despite the individual efforts of many, and in spite of the thin veneer of prosperity, the true condition of humanity continues to worsen. I tell you today, that beginning the first day of the new cycle, change will come to our civilization."

The crowd barely blinked. They had grown accustomed to statements such as these—statements that, if coming from anyone else, would appear to be hyperbole. Yet from the moment he stepped onto the scene, Jimi T. had made good on every promise he made, even those that seemed to initially defy plausibility or even logic. He continued.

"I am announcing the inception of *Operation: Restore Spirit*. This is a non-governmental organization conceived specifically to address the present needs of our world. Operation: Restore Spirit will initially be funded in several ways. Firstly, a full two-thirds of the proceeds generated by *Çön Razón* will go straight into the operation. Secondly, in cooperation with The Way of Mystic Realism, all net profits from various event and ceremony collections will go directly into the mission. Thirdly, international grants will be utilized. At this point, I am pleased to announce that, on day one, Operation: Restore Spirit will have an operating budget of sixty billion dollars."

A few surprised gasps swept through the audience. After a brief pause, Jimi T. went on.

"Still, Operation: Restore Spirit will operate as a grass-roots movement in that it will start in the poorest of poor communities, and will focus on each community coming together to pull itself out of its dismal situation."

"Eighty-one of the largest cities throughout the world have been selected for phase one of its implementation. In each of these cities, nine of their most crime-torn neighborhoods have been selected. A center is being established in each of these neighborhoods for our volunteer staff to work out of. Nearly eight hundred *Ræpôi*, or 'Facilitators', who have been trained over the past six months in anticipation of this movement, will not only serve but also live in these communities."

"Each *Ræpôi* will initially identify the nine most influential—and probably most feared—juveniles and young adults in that particular community. Together, they will meet daily over a six to nine-month period with the objective of identifying and addressing the needs of that community. Once activated, these groups will be self-perpetuating and expanding, as those members will now serve as *Ræpōi* in other local communities.

"In the final stage, this corps of *Ræpōi* will serve as the infrastructure for the global re-establishment of order and hope. These centers will become schools for fulfilling the needs of the body, mind, and spirit."

Jimi T. paused and saw several hands raised in the air.

"Yes, Leon?"

"Mr. Expo, will you require all these people to convert to Mystic Realism in order to be a part of this movement?"

Jimi T. shook his head. "No, this movement is not exclusionary, and is for people of all faiths, philosophies, and belief systems. Currently, all the *Ræpōi* are indeed of The Way, and teachings will be offered, yet not required, for those involved. I feel that, as currently only one-quarter of the world's population subscribes to the beliefs of The Way, it would be inappropriate to leave the others out."

Another hand went up. "Yes, Reba?"

"My lord, who will be overseeing the operation of this organization?"

"I will serve as president and executive director for Operation: Restore Spirit, as well as chairing the board of directors. The people you see here with me today will also serve on the board, along with several others. Additionally, each city will have a local board of civic, religious, and government leaders serving on it."

Several hands shot up, which the Mystic King waved off. "Please forgive me, but there is much work to be done, and we have two additional announcements to make. First of all, as I am certain you have anticipated, *Çön Razón* will be releasing its second album, *Bridges*, at the conclusion of the *Kat'häl*. Yet more importantly, I would like to bring to the podium Senator William Maison, who will be making an announcement which I understand will be received with some disappointment, but I do hasten to emphasize that he and I are in agreement on this matter in light of the long-term, 'bigger picture', as they say. With that, I will turn the floor over to Brother William. May the Spirit be with you."

Senator Maison bowed slightly, yet reverently, to the Mystic King as he stepped forward. Taking a deep breath, along with a slight glance towards the teleprompter, he began speaking in a sober-tone.

DOMINION

"My friends and colleagues, and fellow citizens of the world. I address you today as we near the end of a difficult, yet enlightening campaign, at the end of which I had hoped to serve as your president. Over more than two decades of serving in public office, I have felt both your encouragement and support. In more recent times, I have been a loyal dissenter to our current president, William Jennings Lang. Despite our apparent prosperity in recent times, I continue to have a number of concerns in policy, and I would say, philosophy of governance that I intend to continue to advocate for on behalf of the American people, and really, all of the citizens of the world. Still, after deep reflection, along with discussions both with my running mate as well as Mr. Expo, I feel that this is *not* the time for me, or anyone for that matter, to be running against the president in this upcoming election. I am convinced that we are in the midst of a great crisis—partly disguised by our superficial prosperity—but even so, I do not feel it would be in our nation's best interest to become distracted by, or even caught in the midst of, a difficult election campaign. Truly, this is not the time for the worn-out politics of the past, but a time for us to come together…to find some common ground. I will continue to serve as your senator, and in that, I will also dedicate my time and efforts to the Mystic King's most worthy project aforementioned. For these reasons, it is with some sentiments of sadness, but even a greater sense of resolution, that I am removing my name as a candidate for the office of President of the United States."

ii

The thick mist began to dissipate, and Caleb immediately recognized that he was once again in that *other* place. It was neither pleasant nor altogether unpleasant. Just *different* somehow. What troubled Caleb though was that he would always feel deeply conflicting feelings after experiencing the visions. What the dark man spoke of did not align with many of the teachings he had received from his mother. Still, at the very least, Caleb found that he somehow enjoyed having his natural sense of curiosity piqued.

He looked up as the dark man with emerald-green eyes came into his line of sight.

"Bonjou, Caleb!" The dark man greeted warmly.

Caleb focused his eyes momentarily on the curious marking drawn on the man's forehead, then down at his own feet. *"H-Hello Ph-Ph—"*

REQUIEM

The dark man smiled. *"Oh, sha-sha, pod nah. Peace be with you."*

Caleb looked up inquisitively, having surprised himself by remembering the dark man's name. *"H-How come I c-can't r-r-remember your n-n-name when I leave th-this place?"*

The dark man took a step forward and patted Caleb on the shoulder. *"Because, pod nah, I don't want you to!"*

Caleb frowned, and the dark man, seeing his displeasure, crouched down on one knee before him.

"Would you like to see another magic trick?" he asked.

Caleb tried to maintain his hurt posture, but his sense of fun got the better of him. He smiled sheepishly and nodded.

The dark man grinned back. *"Good! Now watch closely!"*

The dark man immediately clapped his hands together not five centimeters from Caleb's face, then slowly opened them. To Caleb's delight, a multitude of golden butterflies sprung forth from the dark man's opened palms.

"You liked that, didn't you, toot-toot?"

Caleb nodded, and even allowed a giggle to escape from his lips. In a moment, however, the smile began to fade again.

"I-I-I don't th-think my m-m-mom would like m-me sp-sp-speaking with y-you."

The dark man frowned, a slight twinge of disquiet showing in his dazzling green eyes. *"Now why would you think that, Caleb? You didn't tell your mom about me, did you, pod nah?"*

Caleb shook his head.

The dark man provided a smile that could not hide the sense of relief which he felt.

"Right now, this is our little secret, okay, pod nah? It's our covenant. But we'll let your mom in on it real soon, as soon as the good Lord Jesus comes to see us all!"

Caleb looked confused. *"I-I thought th-th-the lord w-was c-c-called Jimi T. Expo."*

The dark man frowned. *"No Caleb, that man only pretends to be lord. But Le Bon Dieu will be coming soon, and he's not gonna let Jimi T. call himself that anymore."*

Caleb absorbed the information relayed to him and found once again that it did not match the knowledge that had already been stored in his head.

"I-I'm c-c-c-conf-fused."

The dark man smiled, this time with a slight sense of dissatisfaction, or perhaps more accurately, urgency. *"We'll talk more about it later. Right now, I want to play the body-snatcher game with you."*

In his confusion, Caleb shook his head. *"N-No, I-I don't w-want to to-d-day."*

The dark man seemingly brushed off Caleb's attempt at self-determination. *"Come on, pod nah, you know you like this game. Just let me give you a little hug, and I'll be zapped into your head in no time."*

The dark man reached out, and was about to embrace the boy, when Caleb screamed stubbornly.

"NO!"

The instant he touched Caleb, a jolt of exquisite pain shot through the dark man's body, and he was hurled through the air, landing a dozen meters away. He looked up in astonishment at the boy, and for a moment, just an instant, he could have sworn he saw the boy's eyes glow... glow *red*.

"I-I'm s-s-s-sorry, I j-just d-don't want t-t-to p-p-play today."

And with that, Caleb turned and began to run away from the dark man. As the scene began to fade, the dark man called out to him in desperation.

"It's okay, Caleb, you don't have to go. Don't be afraid, Caleb. Mo chagren..."

iii

Nathaniel sat in a reverie, *experiencing* his own band's newly released album, *Bridges*. Only the album was actually the furthest thing from his mind. He held a piece of paper in his hand—a piece which had somehow been slipped under his L.A. mansion's door only a few minutes earlier.

He had immediately opened the door and peered out across his vast front courtyard, but only saw a fleeting shadow from around the corner. Without delay, Nathaniel phoned his on-duty security supervisor, Solanus, who confirmed that no one unauthorized had been on the premises. So it seemed the appearance of the paper would remain, at least for the time being, a mystery.

Nathaniel had just about given up on what he had been convinced by Siro as to be no more than a wild goose chase. But now he felt more unsure than ever. Too many vexing thoughts and feelings were surfacing within him. Reality was seemingly becoming more and more become a point a view, and he was slowly losing a grip on which was *his*. He looked over the two words scrawled out on the folded piece of paper.

Forgive me

Nathaniel then held up another sheet of paper, on which had been written, in pencil, the twelve steps of Alcoholics Anonymous. It was unmistakable—the handwriting matched.

A close friend had written out the twelve steps for Nathaniel at least a half-dozen years before. Nathaniel was not sure why he had saved it; he had nearly thrown it out at least a hundred times when he had decided to clean out his wallet. Still there it remained, the only piece of memorabilia that confirmed that there once existed a man, named...

Simon.

iv

"I am grateful, Uncle, that you were able to take the time to visit me."

"I had thought," King Cyrul of Kurdistan replied, "that I would be seeing you in the City of Brotherly Love. I am supposed to meet with a man by the name of Bildeberger there tomorrow." The king looked about the small apartment filled with boxes. "These accommodations, they are a bit more like our old village Hallabja. I had thought you were an important man, Daniel!"

Father Daniel Ananias smiled as he sat amidst the boxes, which were mostly filled with books that had been transported for him from the rectory in Philadelphia. The pair sat on the only two chairs available in the small, two-bedroom apartment.

"I believe I am important to God, and that is enough. These accommodations are quite acceptable. Yes, there are many things I will miss about serving in the City of Philadelphia—some things which this small village does not quite measure up to in magnitude. But I do like it here, and I understand that for my particular calling, it is best I am outside of the potential limelight."

King Cyrul nodded, clearly not completely satisfied, but then again glanced at the many boxes about the room.

"You know, Daniel, you could have all of these on a single electronic device. There is no longer a need for all this clutter."

Father Daniel looked about him. Young Phineas had made the same statement. "I understand that, Uncle. But these... these do not require electricity, and they will never get lost in cyberspace."

King Cyrul laughed out loud. "That is true, Daniel! So true! I will have to remember that!"

"So how did your meeting with the president go?"

"Hugh? Well, it was lovely, I am sure. My first time being invited to this country! The president and I, we share much in common. Neither he nor I are very popular in most circles you know."

Father Daniel hesitated for a moment. King Cyrul, noticing his reticence, responded, "Speak your mind, nephew. I have always told you that. Never let anything go unsaid."

Father Daniel provided an almost embarrassed grin. "Perhaps that is just it, Uncle. I do not know that prudence always permits such bluntness. Though I do not question the truthfulness of anything you say, you *are* a leader of a nation. Your words draw much attention, and can be unnecessarily incendiary."

Cyrul frowned. "Really, Daniel, I do not make any claims I cannot back up. And I am sure you speak of my... how would you say? *open* comments on Islam, yes?"

"I do, Uncle. Not all Muslims are bad people. You were one yourself—as was I."

"I have never said anything negative about a single Muslim!" the king retorted indignantly. "My problem is not with Muslims—most are good, God-fearing people who have not been properly catechized in the fullness of faith! Yet Daniel, open your eyes! People spit upon Christianity, provide the world with revisionist history showing the Church in a bad light, and then they frame us as if we are the cause of all the evil in the world. All this, and not one voice rises to say perhaps that these actions are incendiary! Yet I comment on the incompatibility of Islam with the Gospel, and I am suddenly a marked man. Where is the justice in that? Where is the proper reciprocity?"

Father Daniel waved his uncle off. "Very well, then, Uncle. I will not bring it up again. It seems to touch a bad nerve in you."

The king's demeanor instantly transformed, a wonderful character trait that Father Daniel had remembered since his youth. This man could carry no grudge. Any problems or misunderstanding were always tackled immediately. Nothing was ever left to fester. Father Daniel even recalled as a child the somewhat contentious conversation between his parents and his uncle over his taking the boy on a 'coming of age' trip in the wilderness of northern Iraq. Cyrul had won that argument, and Daniel owed his life for it. Upon returning from the six-day trip, they had found their entire village silent. All had been gassed at the orders of Saddam Hussein. Cyrul's fiancé was also among the deceased.

"Perhaps I do have an open nerve. Your president seemed to have the same issue with me."

Father Daniel, in spite of his less than pleasant musings, now laughed. "He is bold, Uncle. Though not imprudent. He has suffered much."

"Yes, he has. But I have to admit, the meeting was a bit more disorganized that I would have expected."

"Disorganized?"

"Well, perhaps that is not the right word. He seemed quite distracted throughout the meeting, having a hard time staying on topic, and he became quite tangential at times."

Father Daniel looked perplexed. "That does not sound like Hugh at all."

"Have you spoken with him recently?"

Father Daniel thought for a moment. "No, I am afraid I have not, now that you mentioned it. I have called him a few times without a return call. Also, really not like him."

"Perhaps," the king suggested, "he is a bit distracted by his love of music."

Father Daniel frowned. "Uncle, whatever are you talking about? I know he is a lover of Mozart, Vivaldi, Handel… but still, he puts everything in its proper place."

"So when you speak to him, he is not listening to his music?"

"Of course not."

It was now King Cyrul who looked confused. "He had his miniature earphones in his ears the entire time we spoke. I would not have noticed it, but my security people informed me after the meeting. They picked up on the signal. He was listening to something at very low levels the entire time we were speaking."

Father Daniel could not mask the fact that he was deeply disturbed by this information. "I...I will have to ask him of this."

The king shrugged. "I do not know that I would give it too much worry, Daniel. As you have said, he has suffered much. Music can be a great healer."

"And a great deceiver..."

10

"Music expresses that which cannot be put into words and cannot remain silent."

– Victor Hugo

i

The Mystic King moved through the crowd with his contingent of more than two-dozen bodyguards. He had come to pay his respects at the Tomb of the Unknowns in Arlington National Cemetery, then provided a moving speech about what true independence was really all about. In the background, yet still omnipresent, stood the Great Prophet of the Modern Age, Tæsír Hoc.

"More than two and a half centuries ago," Jimi T. had stated. "Enlightened men founded this great nation in a bold attempt to achieve liberation from political tyranny. Yet despite their best intentions, it was not a more universal understanding of freedom for all—lest we forget, all at that time were slave owners."

The crowd had murmured in acknowledgement. It was clear that this was not to be the standard 'patriotic' speech on God and country this Fourth of July.

"And three quarters of a century later, a man with an even greater enlightenment, the one called Lincoln, expanded that earthly understanding of liberation as he and a few other likeminded individuals bravely sought, at great personal and national cost, to free these people from their societal shackles."

"But today," Jimi T. shared, his tone gathering strength. "Today, we see that our fetters are no longer of iron or cord, but are shackles of the mind. Our next step, brothers and sisters, our *true* independence, will be when we, as citizens not of an arbitrarily delineated piece of land, but of *existence itself*, shed these chains and embrace a truer, purer, *interior* freedom that no government, no religion, can take from us."

There was a rousing burst of applause and cheers from the tens of thousands gathered. The Mystic King waited a moment before delivering his final statement.

"Yes, today, as we celebrate an imperfect, temporal form of freedom." At this point he paused, gazing across the greater part of the cemetery, "And as I look out at these thousands upon thousands of headstones, underneath which are buried men and women whose lives were cut short, lives that were to have *meaning*." His last word emphasized, with even a trace of anger evident. "I echo the words of John Paul the Great, a true visionary, yet still shrewd in his recognition that the time was not yet ripe for the full harvest, as he called out, 'No more war!'"

And with that, the crowd erupted. The Mystic King placed his hand on the tomb, bowed his head for a moment, then turned with his contingent to exit the scene.

He was no more than five meters from his limousine, with the Prophet only two steps behind, when the voice of a woman calling out rose above the din.

"SAMUEL!" a worn and defeated Delilah Hagarot screamed out. Jimi T. hesitated, as both his head as well as that of the Prophet turned to focus in upon the source of the commotion.

"That woman," Jimi T. breathed.

The Tæsír instantly sized up the situation. "I will attend to her."

Jimi T. took the last step, ducking into the limousine as the Prophet moved with an easily discernable gentle smile of sad compassion towards this clearly delusional woman. Several of the security contingent moved with him.

"It's you, isn't it, Samuel?" she continued to scream. "I know it is! Don't run from me, Samuel, I'm your—"

But the Prophet, and father to her only son, was upon her and drew her in with a strong embrace.

"Be at peace, my dear," he whispered. "And forgive an old lover. Our son is dead, dear Delilah. He was killed at that concert years ago. Men of power have covered this reality for their own self-interest... and I could not bear myself to tell you."

Delilah's bloodshot eyes stared incredulously at her one-time lover.

REQUIEM

"No!" she cried in disbelief as she pushed away from him. "I don't believe you. Ever since I've known you, you have been a li—"

But at that, the Prophet placed his loving hand upon this tortured woman's forehead, and she collapsed into his arms.

ii

Nathaniel continued to battle an interior numbness which he was unable to shake for any extended period of time. Though in reality, he was not expending too much effort in this direction—in the brief moments of release from this absence of emotional sensation, he would experience a wave of intense anxiety, with seeds of deep insecurity, even regret, sweeping over him. He was counting on the second world tour of *Çön Razón*, which was to begin in less than seventy-two hours at a still undisclosed location, to shake him of this psychological funk.

He was still able to maintain a fairly congenial expression at this 'device imaging' session with many of his adoring fans. The use of handwritten autographs and signings of albums/CDs was all but dead. In this newfangled trend—as *e*Albums were not physical things—each fan would hold out their *iBerry* or their MSES portable music device, and Nathaniel would place his thumb upon it. While their device was providing a permanent record that they had actually met this celebrity, a digital photo from each of the many public surveillance cameras within a thirty-meter radius would be taken and saved on the device.

It did invigorate him, at least to some degree, as the multitude of fans reminded him of his worth as a human being, something he found himself questioning at times.

If all these people want to be with me, then I must not be all that bad.

A monitor had been set up for him as he sat on one side of the table which separated him from the line of fans, where he could see a multi-angled collage of shots being downloaded into the devices of his adoring fans.

Nathaniel continued to maintain a friendly smile as each fan had no more than five seconds of his time before being whisked away. Nearly all blurted out something they had clearly prepared for the time frame given, but most reflected their unwavering belief that they were his 'biggest fan'.

After having moved through a thousand or so people, Nathan glanced over at the monitor and suddenly had to draw on all of his energy to prevent a gasp from escaping his mouth.

There on the screen, sitting next to him, was none other than Joey Escario. His neck had bruises indicative of strangulation.

Nathaniel jerked his head to the left. The chair was empty.

"Is everything okay, Brother Nathaniel?" a young girl before him inquired.

"Please keep moving, miss," Masias encouraged from behind Nathaniel.

What the——?

The next fan stepped forward and held out his *iBerry*. Nathaniel strained to keep his composure as he glanced at the monitor out of the corner of his eye. In the same chair which had appeared to hold Joey, in the image now sat Jonathan, the majority of his body charred.

"What's happening?"

Masias leaned forward and whispered into his ear, "Master Nathan, shall we bring this to a close?"

The Phoenix.

The name of his single-event band rang out in his head, as his eyes suddenly locked onto a figure in the back corner of the room.

Simon!

His heart was now racing. As the figure turned and slid out the door, Nathaniel fought an instinct to jump up and chase after him. Then, something inside him spoke.

"This isn't real, Nathan. None of it is real."

"What?" Nathan inquired back.

"It is all an illusion, all a vanity of vanities."

"I don't understand."

"None of them are with you; you are all alone."

REQUIEM

iii

Officer Bud Petrall flashed his lights and pulled his law enforcement vehicle over to the side of the road. He almost never got to do this anymore—with the *i-Nav* system now in every car by law, accidents, speeding, and most other moving violations were a thing of the past. He completely acknowledged that this was a good thing. Tens of thousands of lives were saved each year from automobile accidents, and people were actually able to get almost anywhere significantly quicker, as now sixty-percent of the vehicles also had the *autopilot* feature (it would be nationally mandated for all vehicles within three years) which allowed a national centralized travel system to coordinate all ground traffic. Truly, the only traffic accidents that *did* take place in these times were always with the manual drivers, and they almost always involved them tampering with the *i-Nav* system, not liking, apparently, to relinquish control.

Bud was pretty certain that that was the case with the Lexus Z-10 he had just pulled over. It was the newest model, so it would certainly have to have both the *i-Nav* system and the *autopilot* standard feature. Yet somehow, the vehicle's *e-VIN signature* was not being picked up by the *e-Cop* system. What was more, Bud was unable to shut the car's engine off from his police vehicle. He placed a cautious hand on his weapon as he stepped from his vehicle and walked up to the side of the Lexus Z-10. The window was already starting to lower.

"Please get out of the car, sir. Keep you hands where I can see them as you do so."

The man began to open the door and step out. "No need to get your panties in a bind, pig—ahh, *Bud?*"

Office Petrall was taken by surprise. "How do you know my—?"

"It's me, Nick! You remember, your old buddy from the Afghan quagmire."

Bud's adrenalin rush quickly dissipated. "Nick? Nick Orieton? Wow, where have you been?"

Orieton chuckled as they did the one-hand-shake-one-hand-back-pat embrace. "To the heavens and back, man. Life has been good to me."

Bud looked at the car momentarily. It was one of the most expensive on the market. "Yeah, I would say it sure looks like it. I pulled you over because your car didn't have an *e-Vin signature* In fact, I couldn't even turn it off. That's not a good thing, Nick."

Nick Orieton smiled. "No worries, Bud. Just run my retinal scan for your background check. You'll see."

Bud was slightly confused but lifted his scanner to within a decimeter of his old friend's eyes. Immediately an unfamiliar screen came across his monitor.

Nicholas Foster Orieton

International Dignitary – Ræpōi

Operation: Restore Spirit

Full Diplomatic Immunity Status

DO NOT DETAIN!

"Now, I have never seen that before," Bud mused, then looked back to his old friend. "When did Operation: Restore Spirit get so much clout?"

Nick raised his right hand, showing the Seal on its back. "Membership has its privileges, my friend."

"So you're working for Jimi T. Expo?"

Nick smiled proudly. "Yup, the very same, and our former benefactor. That small side-job back in Pergamum—which I am eternally grateful that you pulled me into—that was a real springboard for my life."

Bud didn't even attempt to mask the expression of dismay on his face. His voice became weak. "Nick, a boy was killed at that concert. Another was maimed for life, you can't—"

"Collateral damage, my friend. We dealt with enough of that in the Seals. You weren't so squeamish back then, brother."

Bud shook his head. "That was different. We were at war."

"Wake up, buddy. The world *is* at war, and has been at war since the decay of the *Physical Entity* began, and it will remain at war so long as these two *Dishalǎk* continue to wreak havoc and mislead the masses. You have to look past that inconsequential loss of life. Look at the good that Jimi T. has brought from that!"

REQUIEM

"The end doesn't justify the means, Nick."

Nick glared at his friend. "That sounds suspiciously like some outdated religionist philosophy, brother. Did you, somewhere in all the fallout after the Pergamum job, become a Christian?"

Bud looked down. Yes, that event had drawn him into some deep soul-searching, from which he emerged recapturing the Christian Faith of his pre-teen years. The good counsel and warm re-acceptance of his pastor facilitated the transformation. Still, Bud considered his beliefs to be a private matter, and was still uncomfortable speaking of them.

"Well, as a matter of fact, Nick... ummm... Yeah... yeah, I am a Christian."

Nick sneered. "Yeah, it figures. Listen, Bud, a word to the wise, check into The Way. I'm happier than I've ever been. I'm truly free! I harm no one, and then do what I want. No artificial shackles of moralistic norms, no guilt, no regrets. We're in the midst of the *Neöret*, buddy! A new age of limitless possibilities. Humanity is at the center of existence, Bud, not some invisible, external mythological creature that rewards us when we do what he wants and punishes us if we don't."

Bud continued to have a difficult time making eye contact with his old friend. He didn't know how to respond. The smarter members of his parish would know what to say. They would be bold, they would not have the fear and doubt which were starting to wrap their tentacles around Bud's insides.

Lord, help me!

Nick Orieton suddenly blinked, his diatribe swiftly diminishing. He was momentarily at a loss for words. He looked curiously at Bud Petrall, his eyes momentarily narrowing, then transforming to a gaze of concern. Nonetheless, Nick was unable to hide the mildly disgusted tone in his voice.

"Listen, Bud, all I'm asking is, do you want to be confused and bitter for the rest of your life? You want to cling to your religion," he suddenly dropped his eyes to Bud's sidearm, "and your guns for that matter? Hey, that's your call. But trust me, when the day of *Kat'häl* comes, it's going to be a really bad day for your kind."

Bud lifted his eyes to those of his friend, still at a loss for words, yet sensing intuitively that there was a seed of truth—albeit a *corrupted* truth—in what he shared.

"You've got to wake up, Bud. Open your mind. When it comes to archaic religion, the fat lady is singing." Nick paused momentarily, his voice becoming solemn with concern as he met Bud's steady gaze.

"It's the requiem of Christianity, my friend, and the final note has been struck…"

11

He sang as if he knew me
in all my dark despair.
And then he looked right through me
as if I wasn't there.
And he just kept on singing,
singing clear and strong.

Strumming my pain with his fingers,
Singing my life with his words,
Killing me softly with his song,
Killing me softly…

– Charles Fox & Norman Gimbel
Killing Me Softly

i

It had been perhaps the most exciting sensation Nathaniel had experienced in as long as he could remember: a bold, perhaps even dangerous act that confirmed that there was still a spark of life within him. And it was none too soon. Words barked out across the public address system in the Swahili tongue. And Nathaniel, for the first time in recent memory, felt the rush of adrenaline run through him.

Though he never would have believed it, some of the very perks that he had looked forward to when he made 'the big time' had lately not been sustaining his interest for very long. Certainly the attention was great—a constant reminder that he was *someone*, though he had to confess, at times, he found himself wishing that he could go somewhere—*anywhere*—without being mobbed by so many adoring fans. Just a cup of coffee at the local Moonbucks, chatting with a friend…

"You have no friends."

"NO!" Nathaniel fought. *"Not today…that won't work today!"*

The letters, emails, and messages affirmed his value as a human being, and had been great for a time as well. But then some of them started getting, well, just a bit *weird.* Offers of sensual rendezvous were mildly amusing at first—if not downright intriguing. But as their graphic nature, and even gender diversity increased, Nathaniel experienced a sour twist in his innards, which in some curious and unexpected manner created an aversion within him to any form of affection…

"Who do you love?"

"Everyone loves me!" the words actually escaped his lips this time, yet only J.J. Hambon was close enough to hear them. He glanced briefly back at Nathaniel, provided a not unexpected expression of disdain, then turned his gaze back to the stage portal as the amplified foreign voice went silent. Nathaniel lifted his hands to plug his ears, yet instead of the standard roar of the crowd, an audible hush fell across the still unseen throng.

Nathaniel returned to his reverie, reflecting on some of the more recent communications—from supposed fans—that he had been receiving. A growing number were becoming quite eerie—breathing, shadows, whispers. Nathaniel felt some of the same paranoid sensations from his teenage years re-emerge, the anxiety that went along with hiding from the Russian Syndicate. Only this time he was not sharing in the fear with anyone close…

"You are so alone."

But today was to be different. Today was the day that *Çön Razón* defied the international quarantine on sub-Saharan Africa. Despite the still-believed-to-be rampant spread of the dreaded H-virus, Jimi T. had convinced the masses that this was a mission of mercy…

"And a mission of reconciliation and healing," the Mystic King had added.

In reality, Jimi T. had banked on the fact that all international organizations were too impotent to do anything to stop them. He planned out a twelve-day tour, each venue being announced only twelve hours prior to the musical event, after which, the crew would then again vanish into the hidden recesses of the Dark Continent.

REQUIEM

Thousands of Mystic Realism's Anointed—also called *Givers of The Seal*—as well as *Ræpōi* had been smuggled into Africa over the past month, spreading the word and creating fertile soil for what was about to take place. And now, the harvest was plenty.

Still at the threshold of the stage, Jimi T. looked back to his supporting cast and nodded with his typical smile. Nathaniel and his band of co-redeemers then walked out into the theater for their first ever concert under the African moon as the sound of six million indigenous people calling out shook the very earth.

Nathaniel had never seen so many people in one place. A special invitation had been provided, by word of mouth via the *Givers of the Seal*, for all those infected with the H-virus. Not yet fully void of compassion, Nathaniel still had to restrain a gasp as he laid eyes on the hundreds of people in the final stages of the deadly disease strewn across the first thirty-meter-long plot in front of the stage. Even from the distance, Nathaniel could see the grotesque discolorations and boils on their skin and smell the putrid odor of death lingering in the air. He turned away, picking up his guitar from its stand.

"Habari za jioni?" the Mystic King called out, and the throng responded even louder after hearing their savior-to-be speak in their native tongue. With that, Jimi T. turned to Bobby Gandolph, providing the subtlest nod, and Bobby broke into *Çön Razón's* newest single, *Healing Waters*.

After an hour of a truly mystical performance, and with the band nearing the completion of their first set, Jimi T. finally lowered his hands, and looking with wounded compassion upon the sickest of the sick before him, called out in a seemingly frustrated tone, *"Nina Kiu!"*

As the throng fell silent, Nathan looked over to Joshua Ellwood but did not receive a return glance.

Jimi T. spoke again, in a near whisper.

"Unataka kupona?"

There was an audible gasp throughout the multitude, and Nathaniel could see a yearning affirmative response in the eyes of those lying before them. Not missing a beat, the Mystic King stepped off the stage and onto the ground in the midst of the suffering. Bobby Gandolph began to play a note which emanated as a low-level hum from the synthesizer, and Nathaniel looked over to see Jacob Pan, their sensory engineer, moving furiously between the virtual knobs and switches on his video consoles. Nathaniel felt a tickle within him, then watched as an aerosol dose of *Cimä* shot out from all directions. He looked back down to Jimi T., watching the Mystic King as he placed his hand on the first poor soul's forehead, a light crimson hue beginning to emanate from his body.

The wretch reached up towards Jimi T., and Nathaniel could clearly see the Seal, which also seemed to be illuminated, on the back of the man's hand.

Nathaniel looked on anxiously as he saw the modern-day leper convulse. Then, right before his eyes, he witnessed the man's boils quickly recede until they were no more. A moment later, the fully healed man stood and reached to embrace his healer. Then with a touch upon his forehead from the Mystic King, he fell to the ground, eyes closed and lips moving, seemingly enraptured in the most wonderful vision.

Jimi T. looked out to the throng and began moving through the crowd, touching individuals as the crimson hue grew and grew, eventually engulfing the entire scene as far as the eye could see.

The concert consummated nearly two hours later with a blessing from the Mystic King, closing with Çön Razón's popular tune, *A Prophet's Welcome.* When the last note was struck, bows were taken, and Nathaniel's band-mates quickly left the stage. Nathaniel, however, was having a difficult time shaking his dreamy state.

"Come on, Nathaniel!" It was Siro calling from the wings. "We've got eleven more of these. We have to get out before the international authorities track us down!"

Nathaniel gazed back to the crowd, which was dispersing with near miraculous speed and order.

No groupies planning to hang around? he wondered.

"Nathaniel!"

He looked back to Siro, then had his eye caught by something down in front of the stage.

There, in the place where Jimi T. had healed hundreds of near-invalids, still lay a dozen or so individuals, none of which were moving. As the other exiting members of the once great throng seemed completely disinterested in him—as a matter of fact, all of them seemed a bit listless, departing with stupid dreamy grins on their faces—Nathaniel jumped down and, putting his aversion aside, knelt by a young African boy perhaps no more than fourteen years of age.

His boils remained, and the stench nearly made Nathan swoon. The boy's eyes opened and looked to Nathaniel with whatever final vestiges of life remained within him.

"*Yesu...mbona...*" he whispered.

"I-I don't understand. I can't..." Nathaniel felt himself well up with emotion.

The boy choked out broken English. "Why... does not... Jesus give healing... to me?"

It was then that Nathaniel saw the small crucifix around the boy's neck. He looked down to the boy's hand, and as he had suspected, the Seal was nowhere to be seen. Nathaniel glanced at the others lying in a similar state around them and found the same thing.

He looked back to the dying boy. "Because he's a myth," he said almost absently as he felt the first tear slide down his face.

The boy held Nathaniel's gaze, his growing sadness evident as his own tear emerged, then he slowly closed his eyes to this world.

"Aww kid, why couldn't you just go through with it?" Nathaniel was starting to sob at this point. "You don't have to even believe it, just go with the program."

He looked back with hot tears towards the portal where Jimi T. had exited; a wide-eyed Siro was still standing there. "What sort of sick fuck leaves a kid to die just because he doesn't belong to the club?" he cried.

He turned back to the boy, his breathing slowing, tears continuing to fall from his closed eyelids. He glanced at his own markings on the back of his hand.

"Why couldn't you—?"

"*He weeps not for himself, Nathan, he weeps for you.*"

"Who said that?" Nathaniel stood, furiously looking around. Yet no one acted as if they had even heard him call out. Nathaniel again looked down and felt something snap within him as he saw the boy take his last breath.

"I don't need anyone to cry for me!" he screamed. "I have everything! Everything!"

"*No... you know this not to be true. As sure as the sun sets, Nathan, you are alone.*"

And Nathaniel fell to the ground, weeping uncontrollably, no longer grasping the meaning of it all.

ii

"*Mo chagren*, Father. It's my fault," Phineas Savoie blurted out, visibly shaken. "I got too anxious and I pushed too hard. I think I can win him back over if I just—"

"No," Father Daniel interrupted with an unfamiliar sternness. "That is not how I see it. This is not your fault, and this line of defense is over... for us."

Phineas looked dismayed. The two sat in the small parish sacristy, well outside the earshot of anyone else. The most recent out-of-body incident with the boy had implications which had previously not been explored.

"Father! We can't stop! Who knows how many lives have been saved by what we've been able to learn, not just now, but future lives! I've been given this gift for a reason, I must use—"

"Yes, Phinny, it is a gift, no doubt, but I see that, what I permitted to remain cloudy in the past is now as clear as day." Father Daniel looked down, shaking his head, clearly distraught, yet resolute. "I can honestly say I do not know what I was thinking. Yes, it seemed this was a gift from God, given to us in order to have an edge over those who would spell our demise. But in the process, we have violated the sacred interior of a young boy."

"*Mo fet konmprann*, Father, but remember, I didn't choose this. The seizures, discoverin' the boy—that was not just some bizarre coincidence, it was Providence!"

"Perhaps," Father responded thoughtfully. "Perhaps Providence has had a hand in this. And it is true that you did not ask for this gift, nor did you initially seek out the boy. Yet we are still culpable for how we respond to what is before us."

"Don't you think, though, Father, that all things considered, a greater good was being sought?"

"Certainly, I would agree that our intentions were not themselves evil, but that is not enough, Phinny. We cannot seek an end, no matter how good and desirable, while at the same time violating the dignity of one of God's creatures. We stepped over the line with this boy, we used him, we pushed him. That is not who we are, so we must stop."

Both sat in silence, reflecting on the implications of all that had transpired.

"And I must seek repentance…"

iii

It was the twelfth and final concert of the African tour. Luther, along with Eumenes, Cato, Anaxagoras, and Marius stood on a perch high above the throng.

"What is he doing?" Luther breathed in disgust.

"He is drawing their loyalty," Anaxagoras responded, clearly curious as to the purpose of the question.

"He is giving them hope!" Luther shot back angrily.

"Do you not trust the ways of the Anointed, Luther?" Marius inquired, slightly amused.

Luther shook his head. "This is not right. This is *not* our way. Something has changed."

"The way of the Master," Eumenes spoke evenly, "can at times be a mystery."

Luther glared at him. The five now looked on as the familiar interruption of the concert took place, and the Mystic King stepped out among the throng.

"It is not right. This is not as we had understood. All is not as it should be."

12

The Signs of the Times   ح

<<n 1.047>>

Only two weeks after their triumphant return, it is now official that no international body will attempt to impose sanctions on Jimi T. Expo or any other members of *Çön Razón*.

The news was welcomed by many, though the more significant announcement provided is that representatives from the U.L.D.N. as well as several other nations are willing to investigate the claim that the H-virus in Sub-Saharan Africa has been miraculously contained. Reports of hundreds of thousands of infected persons experiencing a full recovery from the disease have been rampant.

If the international quarantine, which most leaders admit has been unenforceable, is lifted, the Mystic King has made it clear that he will send a force of ten thousand trained *Rœpōi* under the auspices of Operation: Restore Spirit into the region.

i

"Well, my friend. Though *my* time in leadership is soon to come to a close, it looks like—with your primary rival bowing out of the race—your next term as President of the United States is assured."

President Hugh Jennings Lang sat on the couch across the room from his friend and political confidant of many years, Sir Thomas Charles Leese. Sir Thomas had moved himself from his wheelchair to a much more comfortable easy chair opposite the president and was sipping the Earl Grey tea that his host had provided.

It was the first time Lang had returned to Camp David, in this newly constructed cottage, since the death of his wife and daughters. Though it seemed fitting for what most likely would be Sir Thomas' last visit to the United States as Prime Minister of Great Britain, it still provided for a mass of unresolved feelings within the president.

"I have to admit, Tom," Lang spoke with an atypical hesitance. "I feel somewhat ambivalent about a third term. As a governor, I was originally opposed to our Constitution being amended in such a way. It may very well be that Washington was right on this matter, not just for *his* presidency, but for the country."

"It's a little bit late for that, isn't it?"

Lang provided a conciliatory smile. "I suppose it is. I just don't sense a certain clarity which I would prefer to have. I have no qualms about telling you that I don't have total... total peace with it. Yet in reality, with Helen and the girls gone, I don't know what else I'd do."

"But you do know what those who would take your place would do."

Lang nodded solemnly. "Of that, I have no doubt, and that is probably the main reason why I stay. J. Walker is a good man, and an excellent vice president, but frankly I just don't feel he has the public persona to get the majority vote. A shame really. I do believe he'd make an excellent commander-in-chief."

"And the House Speaker? He has always been a good advocate of yours."

"Yes, Abdul is a good leader, and I suppose I appreciate his politics—as they seem to correspond precisely to my own." Lang laughed quietly to himself. "But I am sad to say, the prejudicial sentiments, at least on a national level, are still pervasive in light of both the dirty-bomb incident and the Islamic Revolution in Europe. It will be many years before the country would be willing to put that aside and elect a Muslim president."

"Then, my friend, that leaves you."

Lang was about to respond when suddenly, the door burst open, and Sir Thomas' nephew, Adam Moore, excitedly rushed into the room.

"Uncle! They have the *PlayMax Hologame System* in the other building! May I play?"

Sir Thomas glanced briefly at Lang, who provided an expression of encouragement. He looked back into the enthusiastic eyes of his teenage nephew, of whom he obtained guardianship after the boy's parents were slain by the disenchanted remnants of the Irish Republic Militia. The hit was ordered in direct retaliation for his own policies in Northern Ireland, and Leese found himself subsequently, and unfortunately, *frequently*, being unable to deny the young lad's requests.

"Certainly, Adam. But please, the nonviolent games if you will."

"Yes, Uncle, of course."

The boy shot back out the door as quickly as he had entered. Sir Thomas continued to stare at the door, caught in a momentary reverie.

"Tom?"

He did not immediately respond. Was it ever going to get easier?

"Leadership comes with its costs, does it not?" Sir Thomas breathed soberly.

It was Lang's turn to fight back the feelings of loss within himself. Adam was not much older than his own son had been, before the disease had so quickly and viciously ravaged him—not heeding until the last bit of life had been snuffed out of the boy. Lang spoke barely above a whisper. "*That* it does."

They sat there for another several minutes in deep reflection, a habit which they shared, and truly appreciated, within each other. The collective reverie broke a moment later as Sir Thomas returned his gaze to Lang. "I still have nightmares about it, you know."

"The murder of Adam's parents... your sister? Well I am sure. It happened right in front of you. I can't imagine you'd be able to get that image out of your mind."

Sir Thomas shook his head. "No, I am not referring to that, I mean... well, yes... that does sit with me. But that was not a *decision* I made. I'm speaking of the decision to bomb the Channel Tunnel and seal the fate— perhaps the eternal fate—of over a million Muslims. It was the single most deadly act in world history, and I was its source."

Lang leaned forward. "Tom, I mean truly—what choice did you have?"

Sir Thomas' response was stern. "There is *always* a choice, Hugh. I had a dozen options before me, and perhaps a handful of them could have achieved the same objective. But I felt this was the most certain. It provided the strongest message of our conviction to fight on. It was, in the end, the most definitive choice in achieving the endgame I desired."

"Tom, it was nothing short of Divine Providence that you were even tipped off to the incursion. You did what you had to do, truly, for the sake of Western civilization."

Sir Thomas' eyes again welled up. "Prime Minister Dziwisz sent seventy thousand of his own soldiers to their deaths in our defense. He truly believed if we fell, the few remaining free nations in Europe would quickly follow."

"And that was *his* choice. He knew Poland's incursion into fallen Germany would require the Caliph to pull back his accompanying air assault on your homeland. He was right, Poland survived, weakened yes, but still free, as did Portugal."

Sir Thomas relented, again falling into a reverie. He had replayed the entire scenario a thousand times in his mind. He probably would, even now knowing what he knew, again take the same course of action. Yet it did not seem to assuage his conscience to the slightest degree.

"I look forward to a quiet retirement with Adam. Truly, it cannot come soon enough."

As Sir Thomas mused on the situation once again, his eye was caught by the musical device sitting not more than a meter from Lang's side.

"Where did that come from?" he inquired.

Lang surprised even himself with the slight tone of defensiveness in his response. "It was a gift. Just something for listening to music."

A look of genuine concern came across the prime minister's face. "Forgive me, Hugh, if I am wrong, but isn't that one of those devices that covers all the senses?"

"Yes, it is."

Sir Thomas recognized that a certain unfamiliar tension was rising between the two of them, yet still he persisted. "There is only one musical group that I know of that engages in that multi-sensory form of music."

"Can you just say what you are getting at, Tom? No, I don't subscribe to any of the beliefs of this man, nor the religion he promotes. I just find the music soothing. Is there really any harm in that?"

"I do not wish to argue with you, my friend. And I do not need to remind you that our shared faith has declared that all of this is incompatible with a Christian belief system."

Lang's tone further transformed into one of uncharacteristic indignation. "We all have our shortcomings, Tom. I do not pretend to be perfect. Sometimes, we do what we have to do to get through the day."

ii

Annie D. Nesterov walked down the hall to the nurses' station on the geriatric unit of Maryview Hospital. The nurse-in-charge, Kate Thomas, looked up to her with a measured expression of annoyance.

"Hello, Annie. Good of you to make it today."

Annie D. was not clear on what the comment meant, or why she annoyed Nurse Thomas so. Annie had resumed her first vocation as a nurse four months ago following her meeting with Father Ananias. He had been fairly blunt in sharing that she needed to embrace the gift of forgiveness which God had given to her, and to move on. She sold everything that she and her husband had owned, giving it anonymously to several organizations that worked with the poor. She had then started her life over with a modest apartment and her own source of income.

It had now been more than two years since Alexandre's death. Though estranged for some time before his demise, she knew now that, despite his many shortcomings, she had loved him, and she continued to pray for his soul incessantly. Still, Annie wanted nothing to do with the riches she had inherited from him. It was all blood money as far as she was concerned.

And those who live by the sword, die by the sword.

"Anyways," Nurse Thomas continued. "Don't bother with coming to report this morning. You need to attend to that incorrigible patient, Sandy Miller in 33A. Do you know who I'm talking about?"

Annie D. nodded. "Yes, I've met her once or twice, but goodness me, I've never found her to be 'incorrigible'."

"Oh, she's a live one all right. She's real subtle about it, though. I'm sure she thinks that because her husband was hospital administrator here years ago, that she deserves special treatment. In truth, she's a charity case; someone on the board seems to have been a friend of her late husband. I'm telling you, Annie, she is the poster-child for euthanasia. But the stubborn old religionist has no interest in dying with dignity."

Nurse Thomas closed off her diatribe, recognizing the expression on Annie D.'s face as not being one of concurrence. Still, she was not going to ever be afraid or even hesitant to speak the truth. She continued.

"Anyways, she's promised a stroll out by the hospital cemetery once a month to visit her husband's gravesite. We have no volunteers to do it, so that will be your job."

"I'd be happy to oblige."

Annie D. entered Sandy Miller's room and saw that the woman, in her mid eighties, was already sitting in her wheelchair, all dressed to the hilt.

"Sure, Mrs. Miller! You look like a new pin! Who helped you get all dressed up?"

Sandy Miller blushed. "My granddaughter, Chloe, is visiting from North Carolina. She had a business meeting in Trenton and drove out for the night. She came this morning before she had to head out to work." Then she leaned forward as if to share a secret. "I like to look good for Buzz, you know. This was his favorite dress!"

Annie D. tried to prevent her eyes from filling up, though she was unsuccessful.

"Shall we go then, love?"

A beaming Sandy Miller nodded in the affirmative.

Annie D. walked through the gardens towards the cemetery, which was tucked out at the far end of the hospital property, bordering the woods. She had not been there herself but had been informed that it had fallen into disrepair over the years.

"Nurse Thomas tells me that your husband was the administrator of this hospital years ago."

Sandy nodded proudly. "Yes! For twenty-one years, in fact, though much to Nurse Thomas' chagrin, I suppose. She was hired right around the time he was being pushed out. Buzz, despite his shortcomings, was a man of faith, and that just seemed to irritate the hell out of her." Sandy's eyes suddenly widened. "Oh, dear me, excuse my language!"

Annie D. chuckled. "Aye…not problem, Mrs. Miller. You said that he was pushed out. What do you mean by that?"

"Well, believe it or not, this used to be a Catholic hospital."

"You don't say? Well, I guess that would explain the name."

"Yes, they retained the name, probably more due to its good reputation, which they desired to keep."

Annie D. continued to push Sandy Miller along the path, now past the garden, moving towards the small cemetery which was still a good fifty meters ahead.

"So then, what happened?" she inquired.

"Well, you know, they first took away the tax-exempt status of any religiously affiliated organization. Believe it or not, that only impacted the contributions to this hospital a little. Buzz was very frugal, yet very passionate and close with his main benefactors. But it did hurt his ability to get funds from granting organizations. Still, he just tightened the hospital's belt, trying to weather it through."

"Very wise, I'd say."

"Yes," Sandy continued. "But then the economic downturn—you know, the one they called the 'Great Recession', not yet the Second Depression, mind you, came. Well, charitable giving dried up a little more. The hospital board, against Buzz's wishes, felt forced to accept 'Faith-Based' subsidies from the government."

"Well that doesn't seem so bad," Annie D. stated as she negotiated the sharp bend in the path, now only ten meters from the entrance to the cemetery. "Sure…I thought those programs were good, and specifically for supportin' faith organizations."

"Oh, no, my dear, they were a Trojan Horse, and one that would not leave."

"How do you mean?"

"Well, sure, they gave the much-needed money, but it came with strings attached. If you accepted the money, which you almost had no choice but to do, you could no longer offer Catholic religious services unless you provided equal time to more than two-dozen other religions. You had to hire a certain percentage of homosexuals—and every other kind of 'sexual'—and you even had to permit workers from the local abortion clinics into the emergency rooms and OBGYN units to insure patients 'rights' were not being violated if they wanted an abortion."

"Jesus, Mary, and Joseph," Annie D. breathed. She felt her blood begin to boil.

"Yes, we could have used a little bit of their Divine intervention at that point. The final straw came when the law was passed that required all hospital facilities to actually provide abortions, or they would lose their accreditation. Even worse, *all* doctors were now required to perform abortions if they wanted to keep their own license. Well, this time the board stood up, the diocese got involved, and they agreed they could not do this. The hospital was forced to sell, and the eventual buyer clearly knew that, getting it for pennies on the dollar. Buzz was crushed, and over the next seven years, his health steadily declined."

"What… what a horrible thing!"

Sandy Miller nodded solemnly as Annie D. stopped the wheelchair, waiting for further instructions. Sandy's eyes suddenly brightened, though not without the obvious glistening of tears.

"There, over there, that is the resting place of my beloved."

iii

"It's okay, Mr. Freeman, you are going to be fine. Just focus on slowing your breathing… less shallow… deeper."

Nathaniel's home 'smart-system' had made the call to the paramedics when it sensed his heart rate jump to over two hundred beats per minute. He now lay on his couch as two paramedics worked on him with various monitors and other medical equipment.

"I just… don't know—" he gasped.

"Please, Mr. Freeman, don't try to talk just yet. We want to get your pulse and respiration to a more manageable level."

Nathaniel did not know exactly what brought the attack on, though he was sure the constant interior whispers did not help, while the image of the dying African boy continued to haunt his thoughts. It had been several weeks since the African tour had finished, and though he had tried in all of the following concerts to avoid looking out among the front section of the throng—where the diseased were strewn out before the Mystic King—at one point or another, Nathaniel would look up, and see the boy *standing* amidst his fellow sufferers. He just stared back at Nathaniel, expressionless, save the visible tears rolling down his cheeks.

Now, though back in the United States, he would still dream of the boy. Yet at times in the dream, the image would morph into… *Simon.*

"Simon."

"Mr. Freeman?"

Nathaniel looked back to the paramedic, who continued to busy himself. He noticed the tattoo on his neck, a somewhat intricate design of a crown of thorns. The man spoke to his assistant.

"Szandor, can you give me a reading on his skin temperature?" The partner did not immediately respond.

"Szandor?"

The middle-aged assisting paramedic looked to Nathaniel, rolled his eyes, and then with an irritated expression responded, "His skin temperature has returned to normal."

The assistant then looked at Nathaniel again, slowly bringing up his right hand to reveal the Seal on it. He gave a slight nod to him, then returned his glance to his monitors. Nathaniel instinctively looked to the senior paramedic and noted the absence of such a mark on his hand.

"Thank you, Szandor." The senior paramedic then looked to Nathaniel. "Mr. Freeman, as best as I can tell, you experienced a panic attack, which is actually quite common—at least these days it is."

"I felt like I had a hundred kilo weight on my chest. I couldn't breathe."

The paramedic nodded. "That's the way people usually experience it. The important thing to keep in mind is that, even though it is frightening, the anxiety will only cycle up to a point, then release. Knowing that will help make the attack shorter."

"You should take some S.I. supplements," Szandor chimed in.

The lead paramedic looked mildly irritated by the suggestion. "We don't need to be offering him drugs to deal with this, Szandor."

"What are S.I. supplements?" Nathaniel inquired.

Szandor happily continued. "Well, contrary to what my colleague is trying to say here, they are *not* considered drugs anymore. The FDA has approved them as supplements. They are seventh-generation serotonin inhibitors. They just take the edge off. More than a third of the U.S. population takes them."

"I-I don't—"

"I would be hesitant to recommend anything of the sort, Mr. Freeman," the lead paramedic shared as he removed all the monitors from Nathaniel's arms and chest. "You would be better off avoiding any substances in my opinion, taking it easy on alcohol as well, getting some regular exercise, improving your diet," then with an unexpected wink, "and perhaps taking the weight of the world off your shoulders wouldn't be a bad idea either."

The assistant called Szandor again rolled his eyes as he packed up his equipment and left the room.

Nathaniel looked back at the senior paramedic. "Your partner doesn't seem too fond of you."

The man smiled. "I guess you could say we have two very different understandings of reality. He's had a rough go this past year or so, but I would say he's quite redeemable." Then, glancing down at Nathan's hand, seeing the same marking as his partner, he said, "I suppose you two would find a lot in common though."

Nathaniel, recognizing the inference, shook his head defensively. "I believe in nothing, or maybe better put, I believe in whatever gets you through the day—gets you where you want to get going. I don't need any religious crutch to get through life."

The paramedic again smiled. "My experience has been that people who don't believe in anything will fall for everything."

Nathaniel chuckled in spite of himself. "Well, sir, I'd have to say, that describes just about every fan I have."

The paramedic did not respond verbally but handed Nathaniel a card as he sat up on the couch. "Here's my card, Mr. Freeman. I'm only part-time in this position—I live pretty simply. But you can get a hold of me at any time, if you need me."

"You trying to convert me?"

A gentle smile emerged. "No, that's not my job. But it is likely that these attacks might reoccur. Just offering to look out for you if you desire it."

"Yeah, like some sort of guardian angel…"

The paramedic's smile widened. "Yeah, something like that. Anyway, my name is Ralph Tobit. Despite the circumstances, it was good to meet you, Mr. Freeman."

13

Though in a constant state of transition, the *Kôles* was able to maintain some form of cohesion due to the strength provided by the faithful *Řeintûl*, as well as the further evolution of those true Followers of Abraham. In one final effort to unite the life forms, as well as save a multitude of misled Christians who were still considered innocent to the deceptions of the *Ďishalâk*, the *Kôles* brought forth a Great Prophet, called *Mohammed*, who fostered a new interim structure under which many Christians could evolve and perhaps still be saved. This structure came to be known as "Islam".

Sammaet Ď: 1-ծ
Book of Given Truths

i

"The Spirit loves me, this I know,
'cause the Tæsír tells me so.
And if a Christian will not see
Then they'll lose eternity."

Sister Sawlus laughed as she and Caleb sang his favorite song before bedtime. His singing was so beautiful to her, as it did not possess even the slightest hint of his stutter.

Caleb beamed at his mother. "L-L-Let's s-sing it a-a-gain, Mommy!"

Sawlus smiled down at him. "No, my love. It's time for you to go to sleep and dream of the *Kôles*."

The brightness slid visibly from Caleb's face. Images of the 'dark man' with bright green eyes flew through his mind.

"I-I-I don't w-want to s-sleep yet."

His mother looked at him closely, a mild look of concern resting on her face. She had noticed that Caleb had been wetting the bed more and more, but she really had not put much worry into the situation.

"What's wrong, Caleb?"

Caleb looked away, absently picking up one of his stuffed animals.

"N-Nothing."

Sawlus eyed him skeptically. "Come on, Caleb, out with it."

Caleb struggled in his mind. He had garnered the strength a few weeks back to mention the dreams of the 'dark man', and her initial response was not one that made him want to bring it up again. Now, if she knew he was still seeing the dark man in the dreams... even though they were no longer talking to each other, she would be mad at him because the dark man said things different than Mommy. He knew he was still having these dreams because he was a bad boy... but Mommy didn't have to know this.

Caleb looked back at his mother. "N-N-Nothing, r-r-really."

Sawlus was not completely satisfied but decided to let it go. There were too many more important things for her to worry about. She gave Caleb a kiss, tucked him in, and moved towards his door.

"Mommy?"

Sawlus stopped and turned around. "Yes, dear?"

"Are Christians *real* bad?"

Sawlus smiled gently. "Yes, darling, they are very bad. They try to ruin everything we love."

"Why?"

Sawlus thought for a moment. "Because they are very unhappy, and if they can't be happy, then they don't want anybody to be happy."

Caleb pondered the thought for a moment. "I-I think I h-hate Christians."

Sawlus smiled brightly at her son, returned to his bedside, and gave him a big hug. "But Mommy loves you, Caleb."

REQUIEM

"I love you too, mommy."

ii

The day had not been the great celebration Nathaniel had hoped it would be. Having now completed the European leg of the *Bridges* tour, Çön Razón had returned to the United States for another special benefit concert before heading to Asia. Nathaniel sat—still in a bit of a daze—in his chair at the press conference and interview session hailing the announcement that the *e*Album *Bridges* had become the greatest selling music compilation of all time.

Fortunately, Siro Scribner had done the interview and quickly picked up on the fact that his good buddy was not quiet himself today. The few questions he did direct at Nathaniel were pretty routine—questions he could have answered them in his sleep. Yet he found his thoughts drifting back to Simon as Siro's voice ran in the background.

"We're just about out of time, but before we go..."

"Forgive me, Nathan."

"I'd like to ask the Mystic King for a closing blessing..."

"Forgive what?"

"Thank you, Brother Siro. And I speak through the *Kôles*."

"Forgive me."

Nathaniel's eyes scoured the audience. The eyes all seemed to stare back at him with eager anticipation and delight. But as he looked on, a change seemed to take place, or perhaps it was the realization that no change took place at all. Each individual held the exact same expression, and did not waver from it.

"We ask for patience with the non-enlightened..."

"Forgive..."

Their eyes...

"...let us not seek that which is only of the physical world..."

They were blank. Fixated in a phony glint of delight. As Nathaniel reflected on these near-zombies, the lights seemed to dim, and his eyes were caught by a figure who stood in the far back, amongst the shadows.

"May we be strong in the Spirit, and weak in the flesh. In the name of the Spirit, we bid you farewell."

The crowd rose in full synchronicity, bursting into applause and jerking Nathaniel out of his reverie. He felt a hand grasp his arm and help him rise up from his seat. He whipped his head towards the figure. It was Siro.

Siro whispered, "Where did you go there, buddy? I thought we'd lost you."

Nathaniel looked back out into the audience, where the people were beginning to be ushered out of the room. The shadowy figure was lost. He looked back to Siro.

"I-I'm sorry. I just haven't gotten much sleep lately."

Siro looked at him curiously. "Truth is, Nate, you've practically fallen off the face of the Earth this past month. I'm still waiting for that invite to your party that you promised."

It was Nathaniel's turn to look curiously at Siro this time. "I had that party four months ago. You never showed."

Siro frowned. "You would have stood a better chance at me being there if you had told…"

But again Siro's voice trailed off in Nathaniel's mind as his eye caught Jimi T. Expo about to slip out the back door. At that moment, an impulse hit him.

"Are you even listening to me now?"

He looked back to Siro and threw up his best 'forgive me' smile. "Sorry, Siro, I've just got a bunch on my mind. Gotta run!"

And with that, Nathaniel left a dumbfounded Siro Scribner standing on an empty set and quickly scooted towards the back door.

Nathaniel slid unobtrusively into his car and watched as Jimi T., dressed completely in black, mounted his motorcycle. Nathaniel had always found it odd that Jimi T. rarely had a security contingent with him on these sorts of events, yet seemed to manage to slip in and out of any public situation unmolested. Jimi T. kick-started his engine, revved it a few times, then accelerated out of the parking lot. Nathaniel quickly switched off the *autopilot* feature of his *i-Nav* system—again, membership had its privileges—then pulled out, and, maintaining a safe distance, followed behind.

REQUIEM

What am I doing? he thought. But actually, he knew exactly what he was doing. After two years of being in the dark with this figure whom he so desperately wanted to build a friendship with, Nathaniel was going to learn something more. Jimi T. could be an enigma for the rest of the world, but hell, they *composed* together.

After approximately a half-hour of trailing the Mystic King as he moved in and out of traffic on the thruway, Nathaniel had to shake a brief sense of vertigo as he followed him off an exit. He felt suddenly disoriented; he must have ridden this thruway dozens of times before, but he did not seem to recall this particular exit.

Jimi T. seemed to accelerate off the exit, and Nathaniel found himself having to hug the curb trying to keep up. The sunlight was fading fast as he struggled to stay within sight of the Mystic King on a road that becoming more remote by the meter.

The once urban area had quickly transformed into a more scenic nature trail, with a multitude of trees now stretching over the road to form a sort of natural tunnel.

Nathaniel watched as the brush became thicker and thicker, and soon he had to flip on his vehicle's head beams to see clearly. He found himself unintentionally gaining on Jimi T. and soon realized a growing sense of weariness.

"You are my Rock..."

A somewhat surreal sensation grew, as the road began to curve more and more. Nathaniel was now straining to keep his eyes open as he heard his tires continually squeal on the pavement below. The image of Jimi T., though now significantly closer, became a blur to him. To Nathaniel's surprise, it now seemed as if a long black cape rustled in the wind behind the Mystic King.

"Forgive me, Nathan."

The car unexpectedly accelerated towards Jimi T., as if preparing to pounce on its prey. Suddenly, he was upon the blur, and Nathaniel slammed on his brakes, skidding over what he now realized was an off-road trail of dirt and grass. The car came to a complete stop.

And then his stomach dropped.

He ducked as the large black stallion stood on its hind legs before him, screaming fiercely. Fire shot from its nostrils, burning the paint from the hood of Nathaniel's vehicle and darkening the windshield to a sooty pitch black.

DOMINION

The second time the stallion reared and screamed, Nathaniel's windshield shattered into a million pieces. Shaking the shards of glass from himself, he quickly undid his seatbelt and struggled out the side door as the stallion's fire ignited the entire vehicle.

Nathaniel stumbled to the ground and looked up at the dark rider who somehow radiated an ominous glow from atop the stallion's back. Yet it was the eyes that sent a chill through his body. They flamed a bright crimson red.

iii

Hugh Lang stood in his sleeping quarters in the White House staring at the MSES-900s music device on his nightstand. This insignificant item had become the source of an awkward division between himself and his trusted friend, Sir Thomas Leese.

What's the big deal?

How often was he listening to it? He couldn't really say. In fact, he probably only *listened* to it for perhaps an hour or two a day. The rest of the day he just left it on at a very low volume, just for comforting background noise. He surprisingly had no difficulty maintaining conversations with others or doing his work, and the miniature earpieces made it virtually impossible for anyone else to know he was even listening.

"Whatever gets you through the day."

And of course, he would have it play through the night. Though he had no recollection of any dreams, he was sleeping better than he could ever remember.

Still, today was a struggle for him. Sir Thomas had had the audacity to mention the word 'addiction' in their less-than-friendly confrontation on the way to the airport.

"Forget about his foolish comments. You could give it up anytime you wanted. And for heaven's sake, we're talking about music here, not some sort of drug!"

A few months into his use of the device, Lang had found that his interest in the music was starting to wane. But then the second *e*Album had been released, and well, it was simply magnificent.

But Sir Thomas had persisted, noting that a few recent decisions Lang had made from the Oval Office were a tad out of step with his previous positions.

"Pay him no mind! Do you have to fight Congress on every single agenda item? Is not compromise the way of politics? And really, has Leese himself been the perfect leader? Who is he to judge you?"

Yet reflecting back, it was Leese's final inquiry that sent Lang through the roof.

"Have you discussed this matter with your friend Father Daniel?"

"What?" Lang had shot back. "Am I to have the Vatican run my administration?"

That moment had set off an interior maelstrom within him. The truth was, he had not communicated with Father Daniel in months, and now that the priest had relocated to an undisclosed location in upstate New York, he was even less accessible to him. Lang had not been avoiding him per se—he just had a lot on his plate and didn't have the time.

"The last thing you need now is that foolish man moralizing to you."

"What?" Lang had suddenly surprised himself with the last thought passing through his head.

"Just give a listen to the music. One piece could not do any harm. It is only music."

Surely, it would not do much harm. Yes, he would lose a bet with Sir Thomas. He had been challenged to go seventy-two hours without listening to a single song. Lang had not entertained the thought much initially—it had been two weeks since the prime minister's departure—but he had finally decided to take his old friend up on the challenge—about an hour ago.

"One song! Just one song! He does not need to know! Even an addict lets go of his vice only a little at a time!"

"This is ridiculous," Lang breathed as he stepped towards the nightstand. He was about to reach for the device when, on a strange impulse, he turned and looked in the mirror that rested on the wall to his left. He gasped.

The image in the mirror bore no resemblance to the man he knew.

His eyes lacked any of the conviction, any of the wisdom, any of the compassion he had always known to be a part of his soul. They looked empty. His expression was dulled, even blank. When was the last time he had looked in a mirror?

Helen, his deceased wife, had gratefully accepted this particular decorative mirror from Pope Peter II himself when she and Lang had visited him a few years back. She had insisted on putting it on the wall in their sleeping quarters, which at the time Lang had initially thought somewhat odd.

"Look away!"

"What?"

"Do not let weak sentimental thoughts dissuade you! Pick up the device! Listen to the music! You cannot afford this weakness now!"

Lang broke his gaze momentarily from the mirror and looked to the fireplace at the opposite end of the room. One of his aides had built a fire for him on this unseasonably cool September evening. It was a cleverly designed open-pit fireplace, which had multiple vents above and to the sides that drew in the smoke and stray burning embers.

"It is the music which makes you strong."

"I-I am not…" he began to move towards the pit.

"What are you doing? Pick up the damned device!"

"I will not!"

"You must cease this course of action! An eternity of complete and utter darkness will be your—"

And with that, Lang thrust his hand into the center of the fire.

"Ahhhh!" he screamed, but he did not pull his hand out. He looked down into his other hand, and there mysteriously rested the MSES-900s.

"I will not be held!" he cried as he threw the device across the room, where it smashed against the mirror, creating an unanticipated localized explosion.

Lang felt as if a thick layer of mental sludge suddenly slithered away from his mind, and he pulled his hand out of the fire just as his Secret Service men burst into the room.

"Sir, what is it? Are you okay?"

Lang sat, now on the floor, holding his charred hand against his chest.

"I am free," he whispered. "I am free."

14

"Music will save the world"

– Pablo Casals

i

Andrey Gavrilenkov was uncharacteristically anxious as he stepped into the New York home of Mikey Logiarato.

"Andrey!" Mikey called out enthusiastically. "Mama mia! It's great to see you!"

The undisputed head of all organized crime in North America came around from behind his desk and gave Andrey an overdone bear hug. The two sat down facing each other on the softest chairs Andrey had ever sat in.

"It has been a while, Mikey."

"Yeah, that's what I'm talkin' about. It's been *too* long. After what happened in L.A., I'd say you're the last Ruskie standin', ya know what I mean?"

Andrey looked down momentarily. It still sat badly with him that he had not been present to defend his comrades in the shootout. Had he been successful in his own assignment that day—terminating the life of that betraying weasel Mikhail Ostankino—perhaps he could have better justified his absence.

"I do not know that I am *quite* the last, Mikey."

Mikey smiled "Yeah, your talkin' about that Ostankino fella. A strange one, that's for sure. I thought for a while that we might be workin' together. He was always a favorite of Danny's, ya know."

"All too well."

Mikey's expression slowly transformed into a less congenial look. "Hey, Andrey. I know there's some bad blood there, but really—Danny's gone, Vlad is gone, and now Alexandre too. They were all the best. But now, our kind can't afford to be fightin' each other these days. You're gonna have to move past it."

"Is he still around?"

Mikey shrugged. "Mikhail? He's been doin' the Central and South American thing. Making a name for himself. Keeps puttin' out feelers to see if I'd go for some sort of a deal." At this point Mikey leaned forward. "I've never been much into the drug scene, Andrey. I can't think of what else he'd be offering."

"So will you bring him in under your syndicate?"

Mikey frowned. "I don't think so. I don't even think that's what he'd want—ya know what I mean? I think he thinks he's too big to be workin' for anybody. But I'll meet him. I'll push him off another few weeks just so he doesn't get the wrong idea that this means anything to me. But I'll hear him out."

Andrey did not respond but just looked steadily at Mikey. A moment later, his eyes started to fill.

"Whoa, Andrey! What's goin' on there, buddy? You getting soft or somethin'?"

"It is about family, Mikey."

And once again, Mikey's expression transformed. "Ohh, hey, buddy, why didn't you say so at the start? Is it that daughter of yours, what was her name? Sally? Salsa?"

"Sascha. And yes, it is about her. I have completely lost her, and I need to get her back."

"What's she up to?"

"She has been brainwashed by that cult, the one they call 'The Way'."

Mikey's eyes grew big, and his voice made his astonishment evident. "You don't say? I have to tell you, Andrey, a *lot* are getting into that scene. But me? I stay as far away as possible. I'm a Catholic, and we're the best, you know? That other thing, the cult, the Pope says it's bad, so that's good enough for me. That weirdo music too, I mean, what gives?"

Andrey nodded sadly. He found the irony slightly amusing. Mikey was known for attending daily Mass in the morning, then frequenting the strip clubs at night. Reconciling polar opposites did not seem to create much interior discord in him.

"So," Andrey began, now barely above a whisper. "Can you help me get her out?"

Mikey eyed Andrey intently. "I'll look into it, Andrey. I will surely do that. See what I can find out. These cults can be real bad news—don't forget what happened to the Nesterovs—*all* of them. It's a wonder that Annie D. can even walk and talk anymore—the woman eats suffering for breakfast, ya know what I mean?"

"Yes," Andrey responded, his voice revealing a slight quiver. "I believe I do."

ii

"I have come to accept the fact that the Jewish faith intends to rebuild its Temple. This, I feel, is inevitable. I can only imagine what it would be like to lose Mecca to another faith. But I must warn you, the entire Islamic community will not see it as I do."

Ibn Fatimah looked tenuously at the other members of this unlikely council. It would be his last time gathering with this assembly here on the Isle of Patmos before ending his exile. Tomorrow, the once-powerful foreign minister would be making his unavoidable return to the Islamic Union.

Ibn looked to the man sitting on his left, who was obviously very sick and now visibly covered with a number of blemishes. He tried to speak, but was interrupted by his own coughing fit.

"Most Holy Father," a third man began, hastening to stand in assistance for the man who at one time had been considered the most powerful Pope since Christ's Apostle bearing the same name. In the past few months his health had grown steadily worse, trapped by some strange affliction—not unlike that which had taken the life of Andreas II—that left the doctors baffled. Even his countenance's radiant brilliance had begun to fade.

Peter waved him off. "I am fine, Brother Eli. And I must concur with Ibn here. The rebuilding of the Jewish Temple is an unavoidable reality— prophecy must be fulfilled. But I too do not see any way, save an act of the Almighty, in which this can be done without setting off a large-scale war."

"In truth," the fourth and final member, Brother Hanoch, stated, "it would only be the final earthly manifestation of a war started many years ago, a war that has had many theatres and many forms, played out from generation to generation."

Brother Eli looked intriguingly at Hanoch, as if a foreign thought had entered his mind. "Yet this final manifestation, my friend, is inevitable, and in fact, desirable in its own time. Though we must assure that, for the sake of many souls, it is brought to fruition according to the time and plan of *Elohim*. With humanity's free will...and ultimate salvation... in the balance, He may very well permit the deception—along with each individual's *chosen* self-deception—to deepen. "

A brief pause followed while each pondered the implications of this thought. A moment later, Ibn spoke out again. "I must confess, I am very disturbed by what I see happening on all levels. The Jews rallying together in a manner which history has not seen, the Christians dissolving their denominational lines—this could be viewed as very threatening to my people. The will of Allah is not clear to me."

Peter, through his obvious pain, smiled gently. "I do not feel it is the Christians or the Jews that you need to be worry about, my friend. We are all here to rally together against the ancient enemy of the one God, the God of Abraham, whom we all profess to follow."

Ibn, allowing himself to relax some, nodded in agreement.

Brother Eli again spoke. "More than a quarter of the world's population is now under the spell of The Way of Mystic Realism."

"And it will grow worse," Peter added. "Our Lady, in her many appearances... from the French Revolution on, had repeatedly warned us of such."

Though their belief in final redemption was unwavering, the thought of the magnitude of suffering did not escape any who sat at the table. And even in light of their understanding of God having the final word, as the scenario began to unfold, how each soul responded to God's invitation—or didn't respond— the eternal realities were sufficient to overwhelm even the strongest soul.

"And what then, my brothers, of the Temple?" Brother Hanoch finally inquired, sensing that the gathering was coming to a close.

The men exchanged glances, and Peter spoke once again. "The Temple was built to proclaim the greatness of *Adonai*, but also to house the Ark of the Covenant. Until this original Ark and its contents are recovered, building the Temple may be a moot point."

REQUIEM

iii

Hugh Lang sat in the Oval Office listening with delight as sounds of J.C. Bach's *Requiem Mass* danced lightly in the background. He was experiencing a clarity of mind in these past few days unlike any he had ever known Yet for some odd reason he found himself staring at his date indicator on the far end of his desk. It read "September 8."

He could not shake the strange feeling within him. The date seemed to jump out with an unusual sense of familiarity—a sensation even beyond *déjà vu.*

What does it mean?

He glanced down at his right hand, still wrapped in bandages from the second and third degree burns little more than a week old.

A small price to pay, Lord.

The northeast door to the Oval Office suddenly opened, and Vice President J. Walker Shrubb entered the room. The president shook his reverie, looking a bit surprised.

"Well, this is a pleasant surprise, J. Is everything all right?"

The vice president looked confused. "Why, yes, I suppose. I meant to ask you the same thing. You told me you needed me here right away."

"I what? I did no such thing."

Just then the northwest door opened, and in stepped Abdul Ali Kareem, the Speaker of the House. "Forgive me, Mr. President, I came as quickly as I could."

Lang looked back and forth between to two. "I'm certain that I have no idea what this is about. I called neither of you. I…"

Lang immediately reached for the intercom system, pressing it, yet there was no response on the other end. His heart rate began to race.

"It is not prudent for the three of us to be in the same room. I don't know who called this—"

"Actually, it was my idea."

All three shot their gazes to the west door, where an ominous figure stood. All three immediately recognized it as none other than the notorious Tæsír Hoc.

"What is the meaning of this?" Lang demanded. "How did you get in here?"

But the so-called Prophet waved off his question. "Forgive me—or don't—it really doesn't matter to me. But I am afraid our window of opportunity here is limited, and we must dispense with the small talk and formalities. A pity, really. It is not often that one gets to share a room with a Christian, a Jew, and a Muslim at the same time. Oh! The discussions we could have!"

Lang looked uneasily to each of the four doors to the office, all closed.

Why isn't the Secret Service coming? Surely they see this on the monitor.

"Actually," the Tæsír responded to Lang's thoughts. "What they are seeing is something very different than what is in reality transpiring here. I think right about now—from their perspective—an argument is beginning to break out."

"What are you talking about?"

"A heated discussion between the three of you. But as I said, time is of the essence, so we must work in haste."

At that moment, a look of disgust slowly came across Tæsír Hoc's face. "What is that awful racket I am hearing?" And with that, he raised his hand and the classical music ceased. He glared directly at Lang. "A pity, really, Hugh. You were showing such promise." He then pulled a semiautomatic pistol out from under his cassock.

All three men froze.

"Well, no reason to lament what is past. Eternity awaits, my friends! So, really, what I need from you all is a plausible scenario. I need two victims and a traitor—and of course, no martyrs."

The trio's confusion was exacerbated by the calm, even cavalier manner in which the Tæsír discussed his plans. He directed his gaze to Speaker Kareem, looking at him quizzically.

"Hmmm, I'd love to make you a traitor, but really, that would be too cliché, don't you think? We should have a little more fun with this." He looked to Lang. "No, no that won't do at all. Too much of a boy scout—it would be hard to sell." He then looked to Shrubb. "A Zionist... now there is something we haven't had in our country for a while. I think I like it."

With that, Tæsír Hoc coolly turned, lifted the weapon, and shot the

Speaker of the House dead with a bullet to the forehead. The now-former U.S. Representative slumped to the floor. The so-called Prophet then turned to Lang, pointing the pistol directly at him.

"Yes, I know, a little primitive. I'd prefer to see you suffer a bit. But I digress! We will do our best to dream up some scandal in your past that will stick. Perhaps an affair with Mrs. Shrubb? Perhaps a deep-seated, yet well-concealed anti-Semitic streak?"

Tæsír Hoc inhaled deeply, as one who was savoring every moment of the event, and truly, he was. Shrubb, off to his left, found himself literally unable to move, or even speak.

"No matter," the Tæsír finished. "People are fickle. They will believe whatever we tell them, and as they each discover the soothing indulgences of a virtual smorgasbord of carnal allurements, they really won't even care. Goodbye, Mr. President. You have been quite a thorn in our side, but your time has come."

"So be it," Lang responded solemnly, as he made the Sign of the Cross and closed his eyes for the final time in this world.

The second shot rang out as the Secret Service agents burst into the Oval Office from three different doors. They had seen the argument break out only moments before and were unable to respond quickly enough when they witnessed the vice president brandish a firearm on the monitor.

"Freeze!" the lead agent called out as the dazed and confused J. Walker Shrubb unwittingly raised the pistol he now found in his hand—to his misfortune—in the direction of the lead agent.

Five shots rang out simultaneously, not a single one missing its mark.

15

WASHINGTON, D.C. — William Maison was sworn in yesterday as the new President of the United States of America following the assassination of President Hugh Jennings Lang. Lang, along with the House Speaker, Abdul Ali Kareem, was murdered by then vice president, J. Walker Shrubb. Shrubb was shot and killed on the scene after he attempted to fire on the Secret Service agents who stormed the Oval Office.

Lang remained in a coma for three days before being declared brain dead. Kareem was declared dead on the scene when paramedics arrived.

The final determination of motive has not yet been formally established, but sources inside of the investigation, speaking on the condition of anonymity, stated that Shrubb was acting under both religious and personal motives. According to these sources, Shrubb was part of a clandestine Zionist movement consisting of wealthy Jewish religionists seeking to dispel all non-Jews from the entirety of Palestine. In a communiqué discovered dating back more that two decades, responsibility was claimed by the same group for the destruction of the Dome of the Rock on Mount Moriah (Jerusalem), previously thought to be the result of a naturally occurring earthquake.

The same sources cited "unequivocal evidence" that Hugh Lang learned of Shrubb's involvement with the organization, and having apparently himself misappropriated campaign funds due to a previously undisclosed gambling addiction, sought to extort the needed funds from his vice president, threatening to expose him if he did not comply.

REQUIEM

i

President William Maison glanced at the teleprompter before looking directly into the camera.

The voice came through his ear monitor. "We are on in three... two... one..."

"Citizens of the United States of America, and members of the world community. I speak to you today following one of the darkest days of our nation's history. I have just presided at the funeral of three of my esteemed colleagues. Yes, we were often on opposite ends of the political spectrum, but that never hindered our respect for each other, our willingness to work together for the common good, or even our friendship. I can tell you with all sincerity, I will miss them dearly."

All watched as the newly installed president appeared to be momentarily overcome with emotion. Siro, in the back room, instructed the operator of the teleprompter to pause it. He had spent hours working on this speech with the new president, which also included a good amount of input from Mr. Bildeberger, the reclusive owner of *The Signs of the Times*. After a brief hesitation, Maison carried on.

"Nonetheless, I have no doubt that Hugh would want us to persevere, in spite of all this. It was not in my wildest imagination to move into this presidency at this time—and certainly not in this manner. Yet we must always respond to the circumstances presented to us. There is much sadness in our land right now, and not without a certain level of uncertainty and anxiety. I hope today to restore that confidence, though not by simply trying to repeat or even fulfill the policies of the previous administration. As much as we have enjoyed relative prosperity in our country these past years, after receiving some incredibly sobering news from both our own advisors as well as those of the previous administration, it appears that—with all due respect to my predecessor and with utmost regard for his positive intentions—despite pretty packaging, internally we are moving towards the precipice of a crisis that requires swift action to reverse the trends which are leading us there."

Siro took a deep breath, here it was about to be spelled out. Here was where the new policies were to be sold to the American people. Yet he felt confident that they would be well received by the masses. He also had no doubt that his news agency would be singing the highest praises for these new initiatives—24/7 if need be. Most certainly there would be holdouts and critics, simply out of fear and ignorance. Their attacks would be drowned out in a flurry of media productions and common acclaim—for the good of the people, of course.

"The world is changing, and we must change with it. So today, in conjunction with both houses of Congress, I announce three initiatives that will be effective immediately which will truly transform our nation—and perhaps our world—for the new age upon us.

"First, for too long our nation, and more accurately, our government, has horded the fruits of its prosperity—especially over the past six years. No more. In the name of justice, it is this administration's directive that we spread the wealth. First, to the American people. So beginning next month, each man, woman, and child in the United States will receive a check for the previous month's royalties from domestic oil production as well as proceeds from the sales of the hydrogen engine. We anticipate each check will amount to the equivalent of one and a half times the average citizen's current salary.

"Second, we will bring the unemployment rate to zero by reinvesting fully in all U.S. industry, and guaranteeing a job for every able-bodied American. In this, and due to the proceeds which all will already receive, we will shorten the national workweek to three six-hour days across a six-day week. There will be four concurrent work-shifts each day, so that, even though each employee will work only three shifts in a six-day week, American industry itself will be in constant labor, maintaining efficiency and leadership in the world, yet dispensing with the traditional competitiveness in exchange for true world cooperation. We will remove the outdated seventh day of so-called 'rest' from the week, as everyone will have three staggered days of rest weekly, in addition to shorter shifts. We will become a more efficient nation, with citizens who are better rested, less inclined to suffer from stress-related mental and physical health issues, and more available to their families.

REQUIEM

"Third, we are going to open our borders. We must strike down all forms of discrimination and move past the isolationist policies of yesteryear, and even the still-isolating policies of the previous administration. I will be the first to concede that the knee-jerk reaction of my own Independence Party years ago to the dirty-bomb incident was flat out wrong. This embracing of all peoples of all beliefs, cultures, and persuasions will, of course, require a certain courage within all of us; especially the courage to curb all forms of activities and speech which promote prejudice and discrimination, not the least of which has been the continued promotion of outdated religionist mores. We must move beyond this moralism and judgment, and even this over-emphasis on nationalism. We are *all* citizens of the world, called together for mutual liberty, equality, and fraternity. In recognizing this, the United States will rescind our membership in the exclusionary so-called United League of Democratic Nations and promote the establishment of a future, world body that will ensure that the rights of every man, woman, and child on this Earth are fully employed and protected.

"To all of you, in these difficult times, I ask your support in fully embracing this new direction, this new era, this new world."

ii

Father Daniel Ananias and Phineas Savoie walked with deep curiosity through what had been, only six months before, the worst section of Rochester, New York. Father Daniel adjusted his cap slightly, then looked over to his companion.

"Phinny!" he exhorted in a loud whisper as he scanned the local area. "Fix your bandana, your Mark is showing!"

Phineas frowned at Father Daniel, but did as he was told. "I don't like hidin' the fact that I'm a Christian."

Father Daniel shook his head, but could not blame the boy for his naïveté. "We are in the enemy's camp, Phinny. This is spiritual guerrilla warfare. The time for proclaiming openly is quickly passing, but it will come again."

Phineas nodded in grudging acknowledgment as the two came upon a large sign.

DOMINION

"Welcome!"

A voice called out, startling both Phineas and Father Daniel. They looked down to see a young Latino boy of perhaps eleven years of age. He was smiling widely at the two.

"Welcome to our home, I am Umberto. If you'd like, I could show you around our neighborhood!"

Phinny smiled and lowered himself until he was eye to eye with the boy. "*Sa tchob byen*, my man, what's goin' down here?"

The boy's smile turned somewhat uncomfortable for a moment as he glanced towards Father Daniel.

"Ahh, nothing is going down, sir. It's just the *Kôles* being allowed to flow freely within us. We've built a home for ourselves here, but all are welcome."

Father Daniel fixated on the boy's right hand, which bore the Seal of Mystic Realism. He felt a wave of sadness envelop him. Phineas, sensing the strong emotion, turned to Father Daniel.

A woman's voice called out, "Umbertito! Come here quickly!"

The boy turned, then looked back at Phineas with a slight hint of anxiety in his eyes.

"I have to go!" he exclaimed, and ran off.

Phineas looked curiously at Father Daniel, then back towards where the boy called Umberto had run. "I was pickin' up something real unusual from him."

"How so?" Father Daniel inquired as the two began to walk through the former project.

"*Mais*, for instance, look over there."

Phineas pointed to several youths who were painting over a wall of graffiti. Swirls of black and red were being used to create a mesmerizing design which was much more pleasing to the eye than the former gang-related tagging.

"In them, I sense a single-mindedness. In their thoughts, their purpose is very clear, but it is as if they are... sharin' a common will." Phineas looked back at Father Daniel, his confusion evident. "Father, really, if I didn't see with my own eyes that there are a half-dozen or so people over there, I would believe I was pickin' up only a single-person's vibes."

"Like many radios tuned to the same station?"

Phineas pondered this for a moment, then nodded. "Yes... yes, exactly. In fact, I realize now that was what I was sensin' a clear kilometer away as we approached. It's very sedatin', and very seductive."

The two continued to walk, their attention now drawn by several men replacing the window on an old woman's house. In the distance, power-saws could be heard, as everyone appeared to be working.

"And what of that boy, Umberto?"

"He's got a struggle goin' on in him. The more he spoke with us, the more pronounced his struggle became."

Phineas closed his eyes momentarily, then opened them again. "He was called away because the collective sensed his strayin' from their... their frequency."

"The *collective*?"

Another boy approached the pair from fifty meters or so away. He was older than Umberto, and his eyes shifted from side to side. It quickly became obvious that this was not his neighborhood. Before the boy got within ten meters of them, a dozen or so youths came out of nowhere, surrounding him.

"Give it up, brother," the eldest of the group stated gently.

The boy looked back warily.

Another boy spoke. "You don't need to be frontin', brother. You're with the Spirit here."

The boy looked more confused than ever as the group slowly, even tenderly, converged on him. Several boys put their hands on his shoulders, not quite grabbing him, as another pulled a handgun from the boy's pocket. Tears began to fall from his eyes, as the group gently escorted him away and into a nearby building.

"Amazing," Father Daniel whispered. "Six months ago you would have heard a gunshot before a word."

In all, the two spent the good part of an hour walking through the project, greeting and being greeted. They watched in wonder as this once-troubled neighborhood slowly rebuilt itself right before their eyes. Fr. Daniel cautiously looked both ways before asking the question which had been on his mind.

"Has the boy sought you out again, in his dreams?"

Phineas frowned. "Not exactly, Father, but I have honored your request not to intervene—only to be available. I sit there on the outskirts of his dreamscape, and he just does his own dream thing. But I am fairly certain he knows I'm there."

Phineas stopped speaking momentarily as he and Father Daniel provided an acknowledging nod to three young women who walked past them. Their smiles were gentle and inviting, not unlike all others they had met this day. Once they were out of earshot, Phineas continued.

"This I do know, Father. The boy is growin' stronger and more resistant. I sense that there is a greater evil feedin' him. It is not just the mother, and this evil is beyond an absence—there is clearly an intellect behind it. The boy's struggle is still evident, but just bein' honest, Father, I don't know what I'm up against."

"Then you must wait. The boy knows of your presence. You must watch and pray."

Phineas suddenly stopped, hastily shooting his gaze in multiple directions. Seeing his young disciple in this sudden state of agitation, Father Daniel also stopped himself, a look of concern coming over his face.

"What is it?"

Phineas looked around him. "They sense us."

Father Daniel looked around them uneasily. "We're in danger?"

Phineas' eyes closed momentarily, then opened. "No, I wasn't completely right. They do sense us, but they are havin' difficulty reading us. But they have just become aware of... aware of..."

"What Phineas? What is it?"

He looked at Father Daniel with a sudden realization of horror. "There is a Christian among their own!"

"What? These projects are supposed to be open to all faiths."

"MOMMA!" a voice screamed out.

REQUIEM

Father Daniel looked around him as all the neighborhood members stopped what they were doing, then gathered around a woman being held by two men. The woman was sobbing as a boy attempted, unsuccessfully, to cling to her. It was the young boy Umberto. He was pulled away, and subsequently ran into the housing apartments.

"I am sorry," a voice out of nowhere startled both Phineas and Father Daniel. They turned to see a man wearing an armband marked with an 'R' speaking to them.

"We have a community problem here, and we must ask for you to depart so that we may deal with it as a community."

Father Daniel looked at the nametag on the military-like uniform he wore. He was somehow certain that this was not the first time he had met the man. "What has the woman done, Mr. Orieton?" He inquired.

"I am afraid I have to respect her privacy in divulging that information."

"What are you going to do with her?" Phineas snapped in, less discreet in his anger.

"I am this community's *Ræpōi,* and I will carry out the will of its people. She will most likely be shown where she has fallen astray, and be given the opportunity to repent and take corrective action."

Phineas was about to respond, when Father Daniel silenced him, seeing several other large individuals approaching. Father Daniel smiled unconvincingly at the man who identified himself as the *Ræpōi.*

"Thank you for your kindness and hospitality. We will go now."

Father Daniel gently provided a nudge to Phineas, and the two hastened towards the outskirts of the project. Phineas instinctively took one last look back and met the longing eyes of Umberto, who now sat solemnly in the upstairs window.

iii

"Step forward, Caleb, and receive the gift of the Life-Force."

Sister Sawlus beamed as her son rose from the spiritually infused pool of water and stepped up to the Mystic King. Jimi T. was clothed in a brilliant red robe, and her son knelt naked before him, as was customary when one received the Seal. Today, Caleb would become one of the ξ*andide* during the *Ko'nąsarñiä*, a candidate for becoming fully united with the Saved on one's twelfth birthday.

Tæsír Hoc stood to Jimi T.'s left, dressed in his traditional light-grey cassock, while Siro sat next to Sawlus, holding her hand tightly. Upon the altar were several candles, the *Book of Given Truths*, and a second book which Sawlus was not familiar with. On one end of the altar rested an image of a goat's head, on the other, what appeared to be an inverted cross. Sawlus looked to Siro and saw that he too had become teary eyed.

Jimi T. looked directly at Caleb and spoke. "All that exists is controlled by the *Kôles*. Today you will take your first step in becoming a part of the Body, as were the Mayans, Babylonians, Egyptians, and the ancient Atlanteans. Do you, Caleb, accept, without reservation, the gift which is about to be bestowed upon you?"

"I-I d-d-do."

"Give me your right hand, my son."

Caleb hesitated for a moment, the last word in Jimi T.'s sentence still lingering with him. Had his heart not skipped at the sound of the word 'son' coming forth from the Mystic King's lips?

He raised one knee, as he had been instructed, and extended his right hand to the Mystic King. He then bowed his head, as did all in attendance.

"I call thee, Caleb, to the ranks of the ξ*andide*. Receive the Seal, and accept the virtues of Liberty, Equality, and Fraternity, in the name of the *Kôles!*"

"S-So be it, m-my lord."

The brief, localized flash of the Spiritual Entity filled the room, and then all was dark. A moment later, the candles re-lit, revealing a beaming Caleb, the Seal imprinted squarely on his right hand, facing his mother. Jimi T. spoke.

"May I also share with you that today is an extra special occasion. I am pleased to announce that Caleb has been accepted into the ranks of the elite Ńe*ø* M*ị*stè, the evangelical youth army of the *Kôles*."

Sister Sawlus gasped in delight as she and Siro instinctively embraced each other. Two females entered the altar area, one placing a robe around Caleb, the other handing him a copy of the *Book of Given Truths*.

Jimi T. leaned down and whispered to Caleb from behind him. "Go to your mother, my son."

That word again made Caleb's heart leap, and he smiled. He walked calmly to his mother, who now stood in the aisle, arms open and weeping tears of joy.

They embraced momentarily, and then Sister Sawlus held Caleb back to look at him.

"I am so proud of you, son. This is the happiest day of my life."

Caleb smiled at his mother, and then responded, "Thank you, Mother, and rejoice, for the *Kôles* has cleansed my tongue. I am weak no more…"

16

Philadelphia Sports Daily

Sources close to the family have confirmed that Matthew Kohl, last year's second-round draft pick by the Eagles, will not be joining the team, as had been rumored, in time for the playoff roster deadline.

The information provided suggests that Kohl, now a second-year seminarian in St. Charles Borromeo seminary, had not even entertained the idea of returning to the sport. Following quarterback Donovan Jaworski's season-ending injury against the Bears two weeks ago, rumors began to circulate as to the possibility of Kohl's return, whose NFL rights are still owned by the Eagles.

Still, most locals from the "City of Brotherly Love" do not reflect kindly on the North Carolina native. Following his breakout season his senior year at the University of Notre Dame, Kohl stunned the sports world when the still unsigned rookie left the Eagles training camp in midsummer to pursue the Christian priesthood.

Kohl has not spoken to any news media organizations since his departure from the sport, and his family members would not comment any further on the matter.

REQUIEM

i

Nathaniel sat in the back of the automated limousine flanked by his aging security guards Solanus Elias and Masias Moishe. The driver rotated in his seat, having spent the last half-hour reading a magazine, and observed the readings from a few of the gauges.

"We have about another kilometer to go, sir."

Nathaniel had added sleepless nights to his repertoire of struggles. Yet part of him was almost grateful of this, as his dreams had become a constant barrage of bizarre nightmares with rotating characters of Jesse, Simon, and the African boy. He did have fleeting moments of peace, and oddly, those dreams often included the Christian paramedic he had met some time back.

But today was the seventh anniversary of the murder of his parents, and for the first time since then, Nathaniel had felt compelled to visit their gravesite. It felt out of character, as he was not one to dwell on painful sentiments—or at least he did not want to see himself that way. He tapped nervously at the door handle as he saw the name of the town, 'Thyatira' flash on the monitor up front. The car made its final turn, and it was then that Nathaniel saw the mob.

There were at least two to three thousand 'fans' surrounding the cordoned-off cemetery. They held signs, chanted verses from *Çön Razón* songs, and of course, screamed at the top of their lungs when they saw the limo approach.

"What the—?"

"We did phone ahead, Master Nathan, and inform the local authorities that we may need assistance," Masias related.

Are you guys going to ever get my name right?

"Well, how did all these people find out about this?"

Solanus provided a sad smile. "Really, Master Nathan, with your notoriety, you can't use the restroom without the media knowing about it. It is the price of fame."

Nathaniel felt his stomach drop. "Can't I even pay my respects to my parents in peace?"

"I would say at this juncture," Masias intoned, "any peace that you desired would need to come from within."

Nathaniel rolled his eyes as they all stepped out of the car.

Quite quaint, even near poetic, big-guy. But I'd stick with your day-job.

With the assistance of Masias, Solanus, and a host of police officers, Nathaniel was able to fight his way through the crowd, entering the 'secured area' of the cemetery. He had at least fifty meters in any direction cleared, and he trudged up to the resting place of his parents, as perfectly described by the groundskeeper. A moment later, he was before a relatively small headstone which read, "Harold & Violet Freeman" and no more.

"Hello, Mom… hello, Dad. It's been a little while—"

Nathaniel was caught off-guard as he was suddenly overcome with emotion, losing the strength in his legs, and falling face first onto the ground at the foot of the headstone. He wept bitterly as years of pain and unanswered questions came to a head. So enwrapped was he in his grief that he did not even notice the sudden hush of his thousands of spectators.

"I just don't understand it… I don't understand any of it," he sobbed. "It just seems so meaningless."

He found himself unexpectedly craving to be held by his mother, then seeking those days when he played baseball with his father.

Why am I here? Is suffering the only thing that's real?

Amidst a maelstrom of tumultuous feelings, Nathaniel reflected on humanity's desperate attempts to make some sense of this existence, developing grand belief systems that were hermetically sealed within well-presented religious packages. Didn't the fact that none of these thousands upon thousands of sects actually agree with each other prove their speciousness?

"I don't know," he breathed. "This thing that Jimi T. promotes, it probably makes the most sense of any of them, but I just don't find it within me to go down that road."

Nathaniel, suddenly realizing that he was providing too much material for the media by lying on the ground, got to his knees, then quickly stood. Still feeling uncomfortable and awkward, he plunged his hands into his pockets. It was then that he found himself fumbling with something in his right pocket. He grasped the item and pulled out the card which the Christian paramedic had given him. Nathaniel looked down at his name, with a large cross imprinted on the card.

You seem like a nice guy, but you're clearly as misled as anyone. Can you tell me what's real?

REQUIEM

But Nathaniel already knew what was real. His mother and father were dead. Jesse was dead. Joey was dead. That African boy… dead… and Simon…

"Simon."

All those he had loved were no more, and the fact that they were gone due to the messed-up beliefs and prejudices of others did not escape him. They all *could* still be here—their deaths were meaningless and unnecessary. And now they no longer even knew of their existence. When the last cell in each of their brains ceased to function, so did any sense self-awareness. Perhaps they were the lucky ones.

"I have everything…"

"You have nothing."

"…but I'm miserable. I don't understand this existence."

Nathaniel resumed his weeping, this time falling to his knees.

"Get a hold of yourself! They are watching!"

He continued to sob, then stopped suddenly. His expression transformed to one reflecting incredulity. He took a moment to get his bearings, then picked himself up, brushed himself off and wiped his face.

"Who the hell am I talking to?"

He looked around him and saw the many fans awaiting some response from him. As they saw him look their way from a distance, a spontaneous collective cheer erupted. Nathaniel looked back to the headstone.

"This is stupid. I always thought that I'd see you again, but I never did. We made our choices, and now the whole thing sucks. I've got to live for me and have as much fun as I can before I become food for the worms as well."

And with that, Nathaniel Freeman-Page turned his back, moving away from an existence of painful introspection, and once again returning to the life he had embraced.

ii

Mikhail Ostankino stepped off the commuter plane at Tegucigalpa airport in Honduras, flicking his spent cigarette onto the ground while instinctively reaching for another. This was his final destination for the foreseeable future. He had met with the 'powers that be', some official, some less so, in twelve Central and South American countries. All had been arranged by his banker friends—these days, bankers were the *best* fiends a man could have. Truly, it had been so easy—Mikhail knew intuitively how to properly schmooze Communist and Communist-to-be leaders. His network was now nearly complete.

Honduras, on the other hand, would be a different story. Democracy and capitalism remained very well ingrained in this tiny nation. They had accepted many sacrifices to keep the neo-socialists out of their government, and the assassination of their Roman Catholic cardinal a dozen years back not only failed to quell the resistance against Marxist sentiments, it all but killed them.

But things were different now. With the real possibility of losing the United States as its strongest ally under the new administration of William Maison, Honduran leaders were now being backed into a position where they had to start cutting deals. How could they not?

A limousine pulled up, and Mikhail stepped in with two of his henchmen. As he slid into the back seat, his *iBerry* indicated that a text message was coming through. Mikhail sucked in a deep breath of nicotine-saturated smoke, then pulled up the screen.

> Gavrilenkov is meeting with Logiarato again today. Fourth time in the past three months.

Ostankino provided a wry smile. "What are you two busy little bees up to?"

Then, unexpectedly, a second message came through.

> Mr. Ostankino. This is Dr. Sanger's office. Please call right away. The tests came up positive for cancer. Aggressive treatment should be initiated immediately.

REQUIEM

iii

Matthew Kohl rose from the kneeler in St. Maximilian Kolbe Blessed Sacrament Chapel. He had been reflecting on the mystery of how an omnipotent God would choose to lower himself to become a man. The concept overwhelmed him.

It was Christmas day, though no one would know it from the barrenness of the city streets and department stores. Yet today he would offer a small celebration with the youth group of inner-city kids that Father Daniel and Phineas Savoie had entrusted him with before departing for their new assignment in upstate New York.

There was no question that his 'fame' as a former college All-American football star had assisted in drawing in the youth who had grown so fond of 'Deacon P.' as they called Phineas. But Matthew was determined not to depend on this fact to keep these youth engaged. This was to be God's work, and he was no more than an instrument.

And a faulty one at that, he mused.

As he turned to move towards the back of the chapel, he heard the unmistakable sound of bells from outside.

Sleigh bells?

The door in the back of the chapel crept open, and a smiling young Filipino boy peeked through, holding out the bells in his hands.

"Felipe!"

17

New Oxford Times   ~

LONDON — Reports from within the Islamic Union further confirm previous suppositions that the Union is imploding from within. Experts agree that the most vulnerable of the Union's provinces is that of Eurabia, the only province which does not maintain a clear Muslim majority.

The implosion, which some describe as imminent, has the member-states of the United League of Democratic Nations scrambling to prepare for the impending collapse. Though reports are unconfirmed, it is clear that military forces in neighbouring Russia, Poland, and Portugal have been built up against the Eurabian border, while Great Britain has also mobilized its sea and air forces, assumingly in preparation for an invasion should the Eurabian government collapse.

Caliph Ali Bakr, the hailed "12th Imam" would not comment on the situation, though analysts are in agreement that at this juncture, the only way in which he can rekindle unity is through the establishment of, in the eyes of the Eurabian Citizens, an "external threat" (perhaps Israel or even the U.L.D.N.) or provide a scapegoat from within. For these reasons, it is unlikely that the U.L.D.N. will launch a pre-emptive invasion.

This particular crisis has increased the calls for the establishment of a new global entity to engage such situations on a multilateral basis. The United States has been vocal in its condemnation of any pre-emptive action on the part of the U.L.D.N., calling it "neo-imperialism."

REQUIEM

i

"Why can't he be reached? Don't you know who I am?"

Screaming at the holophone, Nathan was quickly becoming unraveled.

"Certainly I know who you are, Brother Nathaniel. And if it were in my power, I would put you right through to Mr. Expo. But I am afraid that he is—"

"Too busy, I know. It's all I've heard it all for the last year and a half."

"Well he has a great deal of—"

"Responsibility? Yes, I know, he's out saving the world and doesn't even have time to speak to his own band-mate. But I'm sitting here writing these stinkin' melodies, and it all sounds like crap to be honest with you. And you know what? I can't even step out the door to clear my head without being mobbed, and he wants me to have this completed by next week so he can put lyrics to it. Perhaps you can tell him I have writer's block?"

"Well, Brother Nathaniel, I would be more than happy to pass that message on, but perhaps if you just took a hit of *Cimä* it would—"

"I'm not drugging myself up to write music! That is not how it works for me, that's not how it worked for Jona…"

There was a pause on both ends, though the holophone still allowed them to easily see each other's expressions. They looked awkwardly at one another.

"I am sorry, Brother, who?"

Nathaniel shook his head. He proceeded with a more subdued, yet slightly despairing tone. "You know, Sister, it really doesn't matter. I mean, at this point, nothing matters, does it? I have all the money in the world, people love me, I mean, who cares if I'm in a band where the members don't even know each other? I mean, really, does anyone care that the music they hear from us was recorded at six different places in the world by six different musicians who never see each other, save for two hours at a time on stage?"

At this moment, the receptionist was wishing that the holophone had never been invented, so her awkward expression would not be visible.

"Who do you love?"

"Does it really—?" he suddenly stopped. "What did you say?"

"I-I am sorry, Brother Nathaniel, I didn't say anything."

"Well, what I mean was—"

"Forgive me."

Nathan swung his head around to look behind him. Nothing. But that was a different voice.

"You are alone."

"I am NOT alone!"

The receptionist nearly jumped at the exclamation. "Brother Nathaniel, I have at least a dozen people whom I could organize a joining party with, really, within the hour. Perhaps I could even send a *Ræpōi* if you would like."

"Forget it," Nathaniel breathed as he cut the connection. He reached his hands up to the sides of his head, grasping at his hair, feeling the inevitable migraine sneaking up on him. Things were unraveling. He let out a scream at the top of his lungs, then collapsed into his couch.

"I'm not alone," he whispered. "I'm not alone…"

ii

"*Asalamu aleykum,*" Ibn offered with a slight bow of his head. It had been five months since his return to Eurabia, all of which had been spent in a moderately comfortable cell while he was incessantly interrogated. Today, it seemed his isolation was to end, as without warning this afternoon, he was told to get dressed. He was subsequently whisked to the capital for a meeting with the leader of the Islamic Union, the twelfth and final Imam, Caliph Ali Bakr.

"*Wa akeykum us sallam,*" the Caliph responded. "It is good to see you *alive* my friend."

Ibn had a difficult time suppressing an instinctive grin. "Would you even say, perhaps, that it is *surprising* to hear of my return?"

The Caliph gazed steadily at him.

"I suppose you could say," Ibn continued, "that the talks with the Pontiff were a bit more *explosive* than had been anticipated."

"You're absence—one which many interpreted as a defection, an act of treason against *Allah*—has caused many problems here within the leadership of Eurabia. Still, I pray that your extended retreat provided upon your return was a good opportunity for... *reflection.*"

Ibn was about to speak again when something caught his eye to the left of the Imam. It seemed like movement, but when he looked in that direction, nothing was there.

"Is there someone else with us?" he spoke, more to himself than to anyone else.

"What do you mean?" The Caliph was eyeing Ibn suspiciously.

Ibn dismissed it and moved on with the conversation. "I regret that my absence has caused any difficulties for you or for the Islamic Union. I understand there is much unrest. I am willing to resume my duties, or any duties which you feel would be pleasing to Allah. I do come with one request, however, from the Holy Father."

"You have now become the emissary of an infidel?"

"No, I am simply a Muslim who carries a message from a fellow child of Allah."

The Caliph was clearly disgusted. "Go on."

"The Holy Father, Pope Peter II, requests your permission—your blessing—to return to Rome and resume his post at the Vatican State."

Ali Bakr was incredulous.

"The sheer gall of that man! Why should I even consider such a proposal?" The Caliph paused momentarily, clearly allowing additional thoughts to penetrate his mind. "And why would the fool even ask for such a thing knowing that it would put his life in danger?"

"He believes that we can coexist."

"As do you?"

"As do I."

The Caliph stood from his seat, came around the table and approached Ibn. "My young student, it would be good for you to take a moment to evaluate your naïve thoughts on this matter—perhaps on many matters. It may surprise you to know that I too desire peace, but I do not believe peace at the expense of truth is peace at all, only chosen ignorance that will eventually allow differences to foment over time, suddenly erupting upon all humanity."

Ibn looked confused, yet still intrigued. "I do not believe that I follow you."

"Is it good?" the Caliph began, starting to stroll around the room with his hands behind his back. "Is it good, or even feasible, for truth and untruth to mingle and progress? Let us approach this simply from logic. Will you indulge me for the moment?"

Ibn was certain that he was being led into a trap, though he knew at this juncture, he did not have much of a choice. "Yes, please go on."

"Very well, my young student. So tell me, then, which son was it who was nearly sacrificed by his father Abraham on Mount Moriah? Was it Ishmael or Isaac?"

"Ishmael."

"You have answered correctly. Yet the Jews—and the Christians for that matter—believe it was Isaac. Both cannot be true."

Ibn strained to avoid any change in his expression as he held the eyes of the Caliph as he continued.

"Was Jesus of Nazareth a great prophet of Islam, or was he the Jewish Messiah, perhaps even the son of Allah?"

"He was a great prophet, of course."

"True, again, young Ibn. Yet again, the Jews see this man as a heretic, and the Christians as the savior of the world."

Ibn was starting to see where this was going.

"And finally—and mind you, these are only a few items given as example—did the Angel Gabriel return and recite the Quran to the Prophet Muhammad, may peace be upon him, or did he hallucinate the entire thing... or perhaps just make it up with the help of his uncle, a Nestorian monk?"

"Why of course, the Quran is true. The angel Gabriel *did* speak to the prophet."

"Very well, but that reality is irreconcilable with both Christianity and Judaism, let alone the eastern religions."

Ibn sensed a growing uneasiness come over him. Though he could not argue the logic, this behavior was uncharacteristic of Islam, let alone an Imam.

"While it may seem the compassionate thing would be to pretend that differences do not exist, they *do*, and these differences affect eternity. They are incompatible, and will always lead to division. If your heart is truly Allah's, you will see that what you desire cannot transpire within truth."

Ibn was speechless as the Caliph returned to his place behind the large desk.

"I do not mean to discourage you, young Ibn, only to make you aware of the reality of our situation. But I do have good news, however."

Ibn looked up, his intended eye-to-eye gaze having fallen into an aimless stare. "Good news?"

"Yes, while you were... *absent*, we have made great progress in learning of the traitor who informed the British of our plans of invasion—that which lead to the deaths of over a million of our Muslim brothers."

It was clear that Ibn's curiosity was piqued, though part of him sensed that this was not a settled issue, and that his reaction was being closely observed. Ibn was about to speak, and again thought he saw movement out of the corner of his eye. He suddenly turned again ... nothing.

What in Allah's name is happening?

"Something wrong, my young student?"

Ibn returned his gaze to the Caliph. "No. Tell me, who has betrayed Islam?"

"It seems," the Caliph began, "that the outsider was—not surprisingly—Abdul Ali Kareem, now the *former* Speaker of the House of Representatives for the United States."

Ibn did not flinch. This would not be a complete surprise, though he was still not sure he believed it. "And the insider?"

"I must admit, I am hesitant to share that, but I will, though you must keep it in confidence. I am afraid that many of our leads are pointing in the direction of your mentor, Mahomet Qutb."

Ibn could not conceal his utter shock at the statement. "Impossible!"

The Caliph quickly raised his hand. "Perhaps… we are not certain that it was him… only that it was someone close to him… within his circle of trust."

"I cannot believe it."

"Very well, I only request that you cooperate and offer your thoughts to those investigating the matter. We do not know how deep this treachery runs."

The Caliph took another moment to attempt to further read Ibn's expression, but he was not able to glean any additional impressions. Relenting, he spoke again.

"In the meantime, I would ask that you resume your post. But please, first get some rest. You seem a little… paranoid, Ibn. I will look to have a meeting in another week. You are dismissed."

Ibn gave a slight bow and began to turn to leave.

"Oh, and Ibn…"

"Yes?"

"I believe I have reconsidered. Please inform the good Pontiff, by whatever diplomatic channels you have established, that I would be honored to have him return to Eurabia. Perhaps it will be just the gesture needed to qualm some of the 'unrest' as some call it, among our non-Muslim citizens."

Ibn had no question that there was an ulterior motive to this sudden act of generosity, but he chose to accept it for what it was. It was the Pontiff's request, and Peter was anything but a naïve man.

"Very well. I thank you, Caliph."

Ibn exited the room, closing the door behind him. Not a moment later, Luther stepped forward from the shadows.

"Quite an interesting conversation, Anaxagoras."

"I am glad you approve, Luther. Though I would prefer you refer to me as 'Caliph.'"

Luther chuckled, yet the sound that emerged from his lips was much darker than that. "So you really want Peter back in Rome?"

The supposed Caliph shook his head. "Not I... it was the request of the Anointed. He desires the Pope in Rome and all the Jews back in Israel."

Luther cocked his head slightly. "I had pondered upon the motive behind that plea. Marius has been quite successful in promoting that end. Zion is almost completely 'pure'."

"And despite Peter's plans, I am sure Cato is anxious to return to his Chair."

"All in good time." Luther smiled. There was still much work to be done, yet at the same time, the final phase of the Master's plan—a phase initiated by the *Illumini* more than two centuries prior—was coming to its fruition in a most beautiful way. Paradoxically, the only person who did not always seemed fully aligned with the script was none other than the Mystic King himself. It just seemed at times he was on a different sheet of music, so to speak. Luther would need to keep a close tab on this.

He looked back at Anaxagoras, his outward appearance now resembling a more familiar image as a light translucent glow beginning to emanate from within him.

"That argument of reason you provided for Fatimah, quite impressive. Not what I would expect from a Muslim."

It was Anaxagoras' turn to sneer. "Many centuries in a cave provides one with much time for reflection. The minds of the already subjugated are so easy to toy with. Nothing like a little seed of doubt to prevent Fatimah from moving forward with anything... *bold*."

Luther was clearly inspired by the sheer cunning of his colleague. "I found the accusation of his mentor quite intriguing as well. Tell me, who was it who actually tipped Sir Thomas Leese to your invasion?"

Anaxagoras feigned as if he was wounded. "Really, Luther, you surprise me. I saw to it myself that the British were informed. Certainly, we could have directed Islam to take over the entire hemisphere at the time, but this path provides much greater sport, wouldn't you say?"

Luther nodded in agreement. He himself was quite enjoying the more active, front-and-center roles he and his brother *Illumini* were now playing in world events. Historically, this was not the *modo de proceder* of the coterie. "So why did you not just kill Fatimah now, as you intended much earlier?"

Anaxagoras once again shook his head. "Why get my own hands dirty with that now? I need him for one final task. Then I will feed his rotting carcass the lions..."

iii

"It is clear she is not going to recover from this vegetative state. Nurse Thomas, please make arrangements for the harvesting of her organs, and inform the next of kin that she has died."

"Yes, Dr. Sanger. But I am unsure of who to inform. Her husband died a year or so ago of the H-virus."

"Doesn't she have any children?"

"An estranged daughter, that's it. She has many siblings—eight, I think, including three priests. Her parents were real over-populators, that's for sure. And with three of their sons in the priesthood, they were obviously masters of brainwashing as well. I am sure though that they would not consent to this."

But Sanger shook his head dismissively. "I do not need their consent. The new legislation is clear. This state she is in is a patent burden on the system, and the potential for real humanitarian organ donation is clear."

Suddenly, the door opened, and Dr. Luke Hilgers stepped in the room. He looked surprised to see the two standing over the patient.

"What is going on here?"

Sanger attempted to be firm. "I have just declared the patient beyond reasonable medical assistance."

"What? This is my patient, and you will do no such thing!"

"I am the medical director of this hospital and have full authority to do so," Sanger asserted, though feeling a certain anxiety welling up within him. "And may I remind you, Dr. Hilgers, that your hospital privileges here are provisional."

"I don't care what your position is or what my status is. You are not going to remove this patient's feeding tube."

"I am not removing it. Her organs are intact, and we have several others who are dying in this hospital as we speak who will be able to live vibrant, productive lives if they receive these organs now!"

"I am telling you, *Doctor*, that if you even—"

REQUIEM

He was interrupted by the sound of a bullhorn outside.

"What's that?" Sanger asked, clearly irritated, though almost grateful for the interruption.

Nurse Thomas walked over to the window, then cursed under her breath. "It's that nut-job, Terrence Aborn." She looked back to the two doctors. "He seems to find some so-called 'life issue' to protest here almost every day. Even the other anti-abortion terrorists keep him at arm's length. He's dangerous. Really, they all are."

Dr. Hilgers was about to resume his argument against Sanger when again the door opened, and this time in stepped Msgr. Craig Ebright.

"Who are you?" Sanger interjected. "No one has called for a priest!"

Msgr. Craig looked at the doctor curiously. "You are attending to my sister, here. I was called in from Patmos when I learned of her illness." He then looked tenderly to his unconscious sibling lying on the hospital bed. "Is there something of concern, Doctor? Has her condition changed?"

Sanger's anxiety continued to rise, though he still attempted to assert himself. "I have declared the patient beyond reasonable medical assistance. I will be signing the death certificate—"

"That will not be necessary, Doctor," the priest asserted, in a curiously serene tone. He then moved to the side of his sister's bed, leaned over, and kissing her forehead whispered, "Good morning, Avila. God be praised."

A moment later, the priest stood up, and pointing to the marking on her forehead said, "Do you see this marking, Doctor?"

Sanger did not like being led into questions which had only one answer, but he still felt compelled to respond. "Yes, a silly tattoo used by the pagan Greek scribes. I've seen it on others."

Msgr. Craig smiled gently. "Well, I suppose one out of three is not bad, Doctor. It is neither silly nor a tattoo. It is the mark of the Christian Elect, and though at one time it *was* utilized by the ancient Greeks, it has been a Christogram used to identify followers of Christ since the early centuries."

"*Forgive me*, Father, but so what?"

Despite the clear sarcasm, the priest did not permit his smile to waver, nor his demeanor to regress. "It means that her time is not now, and unless you are prepared to invoke dire consequences upon yourself, I would strongly urge you to change your course of action."

18

i

Nathaniel was being rushed along the ocean surface at nearly incomprehensible speeds. He could feel the mist of the water upon his face, as he raced along only a meter above its veneer.

He looked to the distance ahead of him as the water began to bubble, and moments later an immense body of land arose from the sea. As if watching in fast-forward, vegetation began to spread throughout this continent. A few moments later the animals emerged, then finally, people. Egyptian-like structures arose from the ground, then finally the fast-forward mode ceased.

Nathaniel set foot in the heart of this now thriving metropolis. He looked around as he saw tens of thousands of people, giving every appearance of living in peace and harmony, going about their business, not taking too much notice of him. Though their dress was simple, not unlike those depicted in the days of the pharaohs, it was obvious that their technology was beyond even that of the Modern Age, only in a much less conspicuous fashion.

Nathaniel looked upon the largest building in the center of the city, which had numerous hieroglyphics inscribed upon it, and one large symbol in the center. He could not initially make it out, but then the image blurred momentarily, and all the symbols suddenly became recognizable. He gazed in awe as a six-story tall 'G' stared back at him from the building.

He looked ahead to see the masses parting, and he soon became aware of none other than the Mystic King in their midst, who now approached him.

"Welcome, Nathaniel," Jimi T. said in his unmistakable touch-of-English accent. *"Your curiosity has brought you here, where it all began. Before Moses, before Abraham, before Adam and Eve."*

Nathaniel looked perplexed as he realized that people were having entire conversations using their minds. *"Where am I?"* he asked.

The Mystic King allowed his trademark hint of a smile to emerge. *"You are on the great Lost Continent. The legends are true. This was a society which possessed the perfect chemistry of the Spiritual and Physical entities. Each soul acts in all the primordial gifts. Were it not for the* Dishalåk, *we'd still be here in paradise on Earth, and no one would be fighting the re-assumption into the* Kôles.*"*

Suddenly, the scene began to alter as the very fabric of the images slowly melted away into a star-filled blackness. The form of Jimi T. began to fade as well, but not before he called out, *"Remember, Nathaniel. You are my rock... a cornerstone to my work and the work of the* Kôles; *that which the world rejected, I perfected. Do not disappoint me."*

With that the image disappeared completely, and suddenly Nathaniel was in a garden. He looked over and saw a young, naked couple kneeling in the distance, gazing up to none other than Tæsír Hoc. He seemed to be instructing them as he played upon some form of wind instrument, and in return, they were offering him praise.

A colossal tree sat in the center of the garden bearing many different fruits. It had a certain familiarity about it. A moment later, he could clearly discern a sound not unlike wind chimes. Nathaniel stepped forward towards the tree when...

Down from its branches dropped a large serpent, clinging to a limb from which it hung with its tail, and hissing in a manner that sent chills down Nathaniel's spine. The serpent looked up and met eyes with him. Horror struck as he realized he was looking into the pain-laden face of Jesse.

"Do not believe what you sssseeeeeeee before you, Nathan," Jesse hissed out painfully.

A muffled scream emerged from Nathan's mouth as the serpent sprung...

And then Nathaniel was back in his room, sitting up in his bed, dripping in a veil of sweat. He had cried out, he was sure of it. He felt a slight pain in his right hand and looked down to see two puncture wounds on the back of his hand where his Seal was indelibly imprinted.

He was losing it.

"Who do you love?"

Nathaniel tried to prevent the tears of mental anguish from pouring out when he caught wind of a distinct smell of alcohol. On the far side of the room, a figure moved in the darkness and then bolted for the door. Nathaniel sat frozen as he watched the figure struggle with only his left hand to open the door, the right hanging limply at his side.

Nathaniel was only able to get out one word as the figure finally opened the door and slipped out of the room.

"Simon?"

ii

Luther sat back in his chair as the holographic images flipped before him. The room was completely darkened save a few candles burning dimly. He took another deep hit of *Cimä* before snapping his fingers to move to the next holo-slide.

In the bigger scheme of things, all could not be going much better, excepting the increasingly inexplicable behavior of the Mystic King. Yet it was his own interior where the greatest discord seemed to rest. Luther fought against the emptiness, an ongoing battle for him, as he reached out, spiritually, to the images before him.

Sawlus, then Caleb, then Sawlus again, followed by an image of the three of them. Of course, this last one he had to superimpose himself into, as

REQUIEM

Sawlus would not be caught dead being seen in public in a manner that suggested she was 'with' him.

Several shots of Caleb made his heart ache. After Jesse, Luther had always pined for another son. Not one like the multitude of weak-minded bastards he had fathered in his meaningless unions, and certainly not one who would defy him, but another in possession of the Spirit. Now he was feeling cheated...

His mind wandered again to Jimi T. Expo, the so-called Anointed One. Something *was* greatly amiss here, though it was not a single act or word on his part that could unequivocally be defined as a clear defiance of the Master. But nonetheless, all was not as it should be.

He took another hit of *Cimä*, and the emptiness became slowly, gratefully, filled with anger—*hatred.* These were his most precious feelings, generating strength, power, and control. Hot tears welled up in Luther's aging eyes, and he stood, threw out his arms, and released a guttural howl which shook every window in the entire mansion. His fury unleashed, the paint on the walls began to bubble, and the candles before him melted to liquefied wax then evaporated in seconds. Finally, a bright flash erupted and all fell silent.

I will not be kept from what it rightfully mine!

iii

The woman stood amidst the smoldering wreckage, gazing up at a scorched crimson-red sky. She could hear the moaning of thousands—those who were not granted the gift of a quick death in this desolate scene. From amidst the piles of burnt wood and broken stone, she could see their arms, feet, and the occasional mangled head peering out, begging for an end to their sufferings—their very existence. A sickening smell that seemed to be a combination of Bengay and rotting flesh filled the scene.

"No!" she cried out. "No, not again! I can't bear it again!"

Then, as many times before, the decimated structure would begin to come to life. Support beams would become whole again, standing on end, and brick and mortar would return to their presumed original place. What the structure became, however, was unexpected. A moment later, each person returned to a fully living and healthy state, and the woman found herself standing in the center of a hospital corridor.

The woman looked down the hall and saw the familiar room, multiple shades of dark colors emanating from it. She could not go there. She would not, and she began to weep.

A monitor sounded off, shrieking louder than her cries. She was initially startled, then panic struck. She turned and ran to the nurses' station.

I can't... let... it happen again...

But when she reached the nurses' station, the woman gasped as she encountered three hideously overweight nurses using *Cimä*, laughing, and taking no notice of her. Strangely, instead of nurses' caps, they wore magnificent crowns. She grabbed one nurse and shook her desperately, but the nurse only laughed louder.

Suddenly, the elevator opened, out from which sauntered three more nurses, yet this trio consisting of ghastly thin, sickly women. They simultaneously changed their gait, beginning to run down the hallway in the direction of the fated room, but upon reaching the nurses' station, they stopped dead in their tracks.

"What are you doing?" the woman screamed. *"You have to do something!"*

But the emaciated nurses did not appear to hear her. Instead, they looked upon their obese counterparts and began to hiss, saliva beginning to fall from their lips. The woman stumbled backward in horror as each of the thin nurses opened their mouths; farther and farther, until their jaws hideously reached the floor. Too terrified to scream, the woman watched as the three obese nurses were consumed by the sickly thin ones.

Yet the consuming nurses' size did not change. They were as thin and unhealthy as ever. They looked upon the woman momentarily, and then chanted in unison.

"One is yet to come..."

At that, two of the nurses suddenly vomited, subsequently falling unconscious to the ground.

Still in utter distress, the woman stood, then slowly slipped away, garnering whatever strength she could find to enter the room. But upon crossing the threshold, she looked upon the bed and saw what looked like nothing more than a gray cast of the one she loved. A breeze entered through the open window, and before she knew it, the figure disintegrated into ashes, which blew all over her and the room.

"NO!" she screamed as she ran back out into the hallway.

REQUIEM

A low hum filled the vision, and then she heard the unmistakable sound of...

A horse's gallop.

Before she could even release a scream, the man on the white horse burst through the elevator doors. The woman swooned with one last thought reverberating in her mind.

"His eyes are blue."

19

"In a world of peace and love, music would be the universal language."

– Henry David Thoreau

i

"Really, Nathaniel, let me call a doctor for you!" Siro pleaded.

"No, no, I'll be okay. I just need to hang on for a bit longer."

The panic attacks had not only continued, but increased in frequency. This was Nathaniel's third today. He had had some success in managing them up to this point. But in recent weeks, each attack was immediately followed by an intense migraine headache which would last for days on end.

"Dude, then take some of my S.I. supplements—the relief is almost immediate. There's no need to put yourself through this!"

Nathaniel tried to fight against it, but as the anxiety began to cycle down for the moment, he sensed the migraine returning. He fumbled in his pocket for the card that the paramedic called Ralph had given him. To this date, he had still not called on him. Perhaps today would be the day?

"What's that?" Siro inquired as he continued to wade through his backpack to find his supplements.

"A paramedic gave me his card... said I could call him if I needed help with this."

Siro suddenly stopped looking for his supplements and grabbed the card from Nathan.

"Well, why didn't you tell me in the first place? I'll call him myself. I..."

Siro stopped suddenly and frowned.

"What is it?" Nathaniel inquired as he began to feel the intensifying throb spread behind his eyes.

"Man, where did you get this? His card has a cross on it."

"Yeah, so what? He's a Christian. Who cares?"

"Who cares? Nathaniel, are you that thick? He's not trying to help you with your pain. He's trying to proselytize you!"

Nathaniel was starting to really struggle as the pain was cycling up to its hardly bearable, yet sustaining, climax.

"Just take the pills, Nathaniel."

He fought against it. "How can you be so sure, Siro? Can't anyone who is *not* with The Way still have a kind bone in their body?"

"You forget who I am, friend, and what I do. I've seen the manipulations and brainwashing these people do. They don't want anyone for a friend who is not one of them. They will use anything as a carrot to lure you into their bigoted moralistic club; I'm not going to let you do it."

And with that, Siro shredded the card into a hundred pieces, then carrying it to the incinerator, threw the pieces in. He looked back at Nathaniel, whose eyes reflected his own incredulity at what Siro had just done, then spoke firmly.

"You listen to me, Nathaniel. *I* am your friend, and *I* care about you. I've looked out for you for almost three years now, and you need to trust me!" Siro's tone became more impassioned as a deep and previously unrecognized frustration began to emerge. "I've watched you slowly become a basket-case ever since *Çön Razón* started on tour, while you've refused to drop your obsession with this 'Simon' character—whom I have no doubt is dead!"

At that moment, Siro stopped himself, stunned at what had escaped his lips. Nathaniel's eyes stared helplessly at Siro, but he could not bring himself to speak.

"Listen, Nathaniel," Siro's tone had now transformed into one more indicative of compassion. "I'm sorry. I guess it's just that you need to move on, you know? You are fighting this false battle here. Take the pills, take a hit of *Cimä*, and take the weight of the world off your shoulders."

A spark flickered in Nathaniel's eyes as his friend completed his diatribe. Siro dug one more time into his backpack, and finding his supplements, pulled them out and reached out to Nathaniel.

"Here, Nathaniel, drop this yoke. It's too heavy, and no man was meant to bear it."

Nathaniel hesitated only a second, then reached out his hand, accepting the salvation for the moment, which at this time came in a bottle.

ii

Sister Sawlus ran her hand gently across Caleb's smooth, hairless head. Though it had initially looked somewhat comical to her, she had learned to accept this piece of the *Neo Mĩstè* dress code. She helped her son button the shirt to his bright red uniform. Caleb looked at his mother admiringly, yet still with an underlying twinge of guilt. He had only a month before finally broken down and told her all about the dreams. She seemed only mildly interested at the time, but had told him to tell her, and no one else, if they continued.

"I dreamed of the dark man again last night, Mother."

Sawlus looked up at Caleb, trying to feign a reassuring smile. "I'm sure it's nothing more than just a former part of you calling you closer to the *Kôles*."

Caleb shook his head gently as his mother turned him around to adjust the cuffs on the back of his pant-legs.

"No, this time I went to him. I told him what you said. He tells me that I am wrong, that this is all wrong, and that you and I are in danger of burning in the eternal—"

"STOP IT!" Sawlus cried out, jerking her son around. The truth was, these dream's of Caleb's troubled her greatly, ever more so than her own. How could she tell her son that she did not know where these images and thoughts were coming from, or explain to him that she was even more afraid of someone else finding out about them?

She took a deep breath, attempting to regain her composure, and held Caleb at arm's length by the shoulders.

"Listen, Caleb, these dreams mean nothing. They are old fears planted in you and me years ago by some sick Christian folk. I had hoped you wouldn't remember what happened to us when you were an infant, but I easily forget that you are a part of me, and we share a piece of the *Kôles*."

Sawlus followed her son's eyes, making sure there was a sense of understanding in him. This was too important for him to miss.

"Now I want you to hear what I am about to say, Caleb. I do not want you telling anyone else but me about these dreams. No one, do you understand me?"

"Yes, Mother."

They embraced, and then Sawlus resumed her task, attempting to tie the black armband bearing the Seal of The Way of Mystic Realism on Caleb's arm.

"We need to hurry. The Mystic King will be here at any moment to take you to the Lodge."

Caleb hesitated, a question obviously waiting on the tip of his tongue.

Sawlus looked up and saw his expression. "What is it, Caleb? What's wrong?"

He hesitated another moment and finally decided to ask the question that had remained in his heart these past few months.

"Is the Mystic King my father?"

A twinge of discomfort shot through Sawlus, which she was sure she did not catch in time to hide. "What on Earth makes you ask that, Caleb?"

He looked down momentarily, then back at his mother. "He calls me 'my son'."

Sawlus smiled tenderly as she attempted to appear unconcerned, focusing on the armband. "I'm sure he refers to many children as his sons; in many ways, I suppose he is father to us all."

It was obvious that this response was not satisfactory to Caleb, but it was clear that he needed to let it go at this time. He would ask again when the time was right.

"I wish he *was* my father," he mumbled under his breath.

Sawlus stopped what she was doing and stared at Caleb. At that same moment, gratefully, the doorbell rang.

She looked up. "Oh, that must be the driver for our lord. Go ahead and get the door, and enjoy your ceremony tonight."

"Are you going to come, Mother?"

Sawlus shook her head. "No, I'm going out with your Uncle Sy tonight. But I expect you to be a good boy, and I'll see you tomorrow morning."

DOMINION

She hugged her son, and then watched with a mild, yet still nagging, sense of discomfort as he trotted off to the foyer to answer the front door.

iii

Annie D. Nesterov stood at the bus station, only meters from the entrance of the autobus that would take her to Pittsford, New York without the need of even a driver. Father Daniel had urged her to prayerfully consider joining himself and Phineas at his new assignment. The boy needed a mother figure in the Faith, and Father Daniel required a trusted associate for the work he was now called to do. She had flatly refused him initially. But as the days went on, with the dark cloud of emptiness within her not lifting, she had reached an epiphany.

I cannot change the past, Lord. But I can change the path I myself am on.

She had sold what little she had left. All her possessions were now in the suitcase beside her. The only thing left to do was to place the envelope informing Nurse Thomas of her resignation in the post office box. Conveniently—even perhaps providentially—a box sat ten meters in front of the autobus docking station. Annie D. noted how it was much smaller than the mail receptacles of yesteryear.

Aye, I must be the only one still mailin' letters all about these days!

This last act was to be a piece of cake. She had done the difficult work already. Still, Annie did not know why she was still having such a struggle now. She could not seem to get herself to move. She glanced down at her feet.

Come now, fifteen steps to the mailbox, another fifteen to the bus. I'll not be askin' any more of yus!

She took a deep breath, and with every bit of her will, she began to lift her right foot. Then out of the corner of her eye, Annie saw something familiar.

A man of perhaps eighty years, though moving as nimbly as a teenager, placed his bag down next to the bus porter on the executive autobus track.

"Spasiba."

The porter looked at the man curiously as Annie turned completely around.

He spoke Russian!

REQUIEM

She could not see his full profile, and she saw nothing more as he stepped onto the executive class autobus, the door closing quickly behind him. The porter loaded the man's bag, placed his hand on the palm recognition scanner, and the bus slowly began to back out.

I know that man, Annie assured herself as she started to move towards the bus, which was now beginning to pull away. She suddenly saw his face in the back window of the bus. It was ghastly white, but the face was unmistakable.

"Vlad!" she cried out, startling not only the porter but the dozen or so people around her. "Vladimir Ivankov! It's me! Annie!"

She looked helplessly as the bus began to accelerate away. The apparition-like face looked only briefly at Annie D. without any discernable sign of recognition.

"He's a dead man, Annie. He died years ago, and Alex took his place."

"Vladimir!" she screamed all the louder as she began to run towards the moving bus. The porter stepped out to grab her, and Annie braced herself for a collision when…

…she passed right through him. She stopped herself, startled by what had just transpired, and looked at the bus fading off into the darkness. The face of the man who resembled every aspect of her husband's one-time boss seemed to almost glow, and she could have sworn a sad smile emerged upon his face. The last thing Annie could discern was the digital screen above the back window of the bus citing its destination. It read "Croatoan."

Dispirited, Annie turned to apologize to the porter but did not find him there. She looked over to her own intended bus.

"Last call for Rochester, NY and all stops in between," a different porter called out. He looked over to Annie. "Ma'am, are you getting on this bus?"

"I-I…"

"Could you tell me your final destination?"

iv

Father Daniel opened the door to the apartment, and immediately dropped his groceries when he found Phineas on the ground in a full seizure.

They were now taking place two to three times a day, and though the majority were still fixed on the boy, many of the visions were now seemingly random people, presumably in need. A part of Father Daniel was skeptical as to the actual existence of many of these people... their activities were dark and beyond most anything he as a priest had even heard in the confessional. With their increasingly dark and consuming nature, he had begun to question the origin of this so-called 'gift' of Phineas'.

He knelt down by the boy as the convulsions suddenly stopped. Phineas' eyes opened, and he bolted up into a sitting position, crying out, "Sascha Luneska! Her name is Sascha Luneska... and she is in great danger!" He turned to the priest, eyes pleading. "We must help her... it may already be too late!"

20

In the history of mankind, there has been one man born of woman with a fully unobstructed, free flowing access to the *Kôles*. This man was called *Jesus of Nazareth*.

Jesus understood the struggle that humankind faced, as well as the strange beliefs which they had digressed into, fostered by the *Ďishalák*. It was he that first realized the enormous mission he would face in order to begin to clear this psychic blockage. Jesus recognized the dangers of the development of a false religion, and sought to enlighten others by speaking symbolically and in parables— attempting to loosen the "psychic sludge" which had systematically built up in mankind's collective minds.

But alas, Jesus was not immune to worldly deceptions. The *Ďishalák* had grown so powerful by this time, they were able to beguile Jesus, luring him into desires for personal gain. They used his open passage to the *Kôles* to further infiltrate and attempt to destroy Her. The *Ďishalák* manipulated Jesus for their own crusade of annihilation, then had him nailed to a tree.

Jesus realized his error on the cross, after he called out to one of the *Ďishalák* for release, and did not receive it. In the end, he was able to salvage his existence, releasing himself from the deceptions of the *Ďishalák*, integrating back into the *Kôles*.

Naamak B: 1-11
Book of Given Truths

DOMINION

i

Ralph Tobit knelt amidst the wreckage of nearly a dozen vehicles on Interstate 5. Accidents such as these were a rarity these days with the National *i-Nav* system monitoring and directing all traffic, adjusting speed and course in each vehicle via satellites, cellular towers, and onboard sensors. Yet today it was clear that someone had illegally tampered with their system, resulting in the extensive carnage before him.

He placed his hand over the woman's eyes, closing them to this world, as he breathed a prayer, pleading for the mercy of the Almighty God upon her soul. Her face was not unknown to him. He saw the Seal of Mystic Realism on the back of her hand—a hand which somehow still seemingly desperately clung to a dispenser of the drug called *Cimä*.

Ralph looked up to see the half-dozen ambulances and police vehicles surrounding the scene, yet suddenly their lights froze in motion. He turned his eyes to the right, then to the left, rapidly realizing that *everything*, save himself, was in suspended animation.

"Quite fascinating, this existing *in time* thing, wouldn't you say, *Ralph?*"

He stood and turned, and there before him stood the Mystic King.

"Brilliant, even I would say. A series of sequential moments, yet moving in only a single direction, and at an unchanging pace. Once the moment is gone, it cannot be recovered. I suppose in that way, it could be considered a bit limiting... even *unforgiving*."

Ralph held the proclaimed savior-of-the-world's gaze, but still said nothing. Jimi T. took a moment to scan the scene, then looked back to Ralph.

"This is so tragic," he continued. "So much pain and suffering— *unnecessary* pain, I would say."

Ralph's eyes narrowed. "What is it that you are doing?"

Jimi T. cocked his head slightly. "What am I doing? I was going to ask you the same thing. The reality is, Ralph, *I know who you are.*"

"Do you?" Ralph responded coolly.

"Yes, I do. And do you know who I am?"

"Of course. You are Jimi T. Expo, the musician and proponent of that nonsensical religion."

REQUIEM

Jimi T. provided his familiar faint smile. "Perhaps you should look a little closer, a little... *deeper*." And with that, he removed his old-style sunglasses, allowing Ralph to gaze into eternity.

Ralph's eyes held steady for a moment, then slowly widened. "It... is... *you*..." he whispered in utter astonishment.

Jimi T.'s smile broadened, "In the flesh."

The two stood for what would seem like an eternity had time not been suspended. It was Jimi T. who broke the moment, gesturing curiously at Ralph.

"So *this* is being about the Sovereign's business?"

"I am here as guardian. I am called to protect."

Jimi T. shook his head. "Well then, I would say your mission is an utter failure. You failed to save the boy."

The words struck like a spear at Ralph's core, as he looked downward, displaying obvious regret. Jimi T. continued.

"You failed to preserve the seed—"

Ralph looked up, glaring, yet still in discernable anguish. "I was bound for a season. I was powerless to help him."

Jimi T. nodded in acknowledgement. "Yes, but nonetheless, now you propose to save another from harm, the young man Nathaniel, and under your protection, he too will perish." The Mystic King permitted a dramatic pause to settle upon the moment. "But there is another way."

Ralph looked back up to Jimi T., who had replaced his sunglasses by this point. "Of what are you speaking?"

"It's quite simple, really. Join me, and together we will not only save young Nathaniel, but the entire world."

"Surely, you do not expect me to unite with you in your rebellion?"

"Rebellion? Well, I suppose that is in the eye of the beholder. But truly, you should hear me out. Since I have been *here*, I have had a... a change of heart, you might say."

Ralph eyed the Mystic King with an expression of amused suspicion. "Surely your Master would not take too kindly to such a concept."

"I am my own being, Ralph, and unlike you, I have relinquished *nothing* to enter this existence. You are powerless against me here."

"What I have given up, I have done so freely. It is the way of the Sovereign."

Jimi T. gestured to the carnage surrounding them. "As is this, apparently."

Ralph was unfazed. "Surely, is your pride so great that you cannot see the eternal consequences to your choice?"

"Even eternity is not a foregone conclusion, my brother, though the Sovereign has tried to present it as such." Jimi T. then lifted his hands in a conciliatory fashion as he took a step towards Ralph. "But really, let us not bicker over such things. You and I both desire the salvation of this soul, Nathaniel, and his ultimate liberation."

"Perhaps we do not share the same definitions of those terms."

Jimi T. nodded acquiescently while taking another step forward. "Be that as it may, the reality is this; I am offering you an opportunity for true emancipation—a freedom beyond anything which even you have imagined. Perhaps my new understanding transcends even that of the one you call my 'master'. Perhaps its path will one day merge with that of your Sovereign."

Ralph held a steady gaze towards the Mystic King. A moment again passed between the two as Jimi T. stretched out his open hand toward Ralph. "I have the power to give you life, or to propel you into the blinding abyss. A choice is before you. Will you choose life, my brother?"

ii

He took his final swig of Mad Dog 20/20 as he sat on the park bench, then smashed the bottle against the building in disgust. This had come to be his ritual whenever he killed a bottle. It was good to get mad every now and then, and there was no better time to be mad than on a cold rainy night like this one.

He stood, reached into his left coat pocket, and pulled out another bottle. It was one of life's great wonders. No matter how many times he reached into that pocket, a bottle would always magically be there. What's more, it was always the *exact* liquor he desired. It had been this way ever since he had met up with that strange preacher a mere three years ago. A little bit of heaven right here on Earth.

He staggered through the alleyway, humming an old tune to himself.

REQUIEM

His eyes began to itch, so he reached up with his limp right hand to attempt to relieve this annoyance. He tried to rub the itch, but it was not sufficient. He needed fingers, and the ones he had that actually worked were busy holding the bottle in his left hand. This was nothing short of Hell on Earth.

After a few minutes of contemplation, he finally decided to smash the bottle—there were plenty more where that came from. Of course, by this time he had forgotten what he needed his working hand for.

He shrugged and then pulled another bottle out of his magic pocket, this time old Russian Vodka—he found that to be slightly ironic—and then staggered out across the street. He walked right past the dozens of fliers bearing his likeness with the announcement "MISSING."

He reached the opposite end of the street, lightly stroked his scraggly beard, then nearly fell backwards as the neon-like hologram came to life before him.

It was a ten-story-high image of none other than the Great Prophet of the Modern Age, Tæsír Hoc.

His heart jumped as he struggled to keep his footing. He hoped he had not cried out, but he was not sure if he had or not. But once he realized that this was just an image and not the real thing, his fear slowly gave way to pure, unadulterated hatred.

"Fuck you," he muttered under his breath. He waited, almost anticipating the image coming to life to wreak further havoc on his. Yet, nothing happened.

"Fuck you," he said again in a voice loud enough for a nearby bystander to hear and take offense. Yet there was still no reaction from the image. A slight maniacal grin, reflecting the pinnacle of his anger, slid across his face as he took in a deep breath.

"Fuck you! Fuck you! Fuck You! FUCK YOU!"

And he hurled his bottle at the image, only to be disappointed to see it pass through and land with a dull thud on the grass behind. He instantly dropped to the ground and burst into tears, cradling his lame hand.

"Simon," a voice called out, perhaps from inside his head.

Or was it? He stood and looked up. There, across the street under a flickering streetlamp, fading in and out as if in a dream, was a face from years ago...

DOMINION

iii

It was the last straw for Nathaniel.

The elusive *Simonesque* apparition, one that had initially sparked a sensation of... *hope* within him, had now transformed into a maddening specter—Nathaniel's own 'white whale', driving him to deeper tiers of dark obsession. Yet after three fruitless years, a small voice inside him assured Nathaniel that the phantom he sought was none other than a representation of innocence lost—an aberration of his own tormented soul.

The distraction Nathaniel had sought in music had also become his albatross. His frustration had built up, little by little, over the three years he had served as lead guitarist and composer for *Çön Razón*. He found himself completely disillusioned with the lifestyle he had so craved all his life.

"You are so alone."

"Yes, I concede. I AM alone... completely."

Nathaniel was rich beyond all needs. He was known by perhaps every man, woman, and child on the face of the Earth. He could have any woman he wanted. Yet, he could not even recall what it felt like to be... to be... *happy*.

"Who do you love?"

And today, when the band announced the release of their third, and as he was now told, final album, *Portals*, all of the pain came together and something snapped within him. This was not a band. There was no feeling of mutuality between the members—at least none that did not revolve around getting 'high' in some form together. In Jimi T., Nathaniel had foreseen one with whom he would form a bond that would rival that of his with Jonathan.

"No, it's Jesse."

Yes, instead of being a crew drawn together by the creative bond of music, *Çön Razón* was no more than a soulless business arrangement. Composing the music had become rote even for Nathaniel—unexciting, uninspired. Yet when all was said and done, Jimi T. would add his haunting voice and lyrics, while Jacob Pan would 'inject' emotion and spirit into the piece. It was so unnatural, but it seemed to get the job done for the fans.

"You are my rock."

The Mystic King's voice rang in Nathaniel's mind as he took a step closer to the edge of the building. He looked down at the back of his hand, feeling his stomach knot up. The Seal was still there, but so were the two puncture wounds from his vision—they had never healed. Nathan's mind drifted to the conference, held only hours earlier, where Jimi T. had announced his dissolution of *Çön Razón*.

"The time has come," he stated, "for a new generation of musicians to step forth, in the likeness of *Çön Razón*, giving praise to the Spirit of the *Kôles*."

Nathaniel had grown to *hate* the band. He had prayed for a way out.

Prayed?

And here it was given to him. Yes, here he was, finally expressing his free will, now looking down seventy-two stories to the various vehicles moving in a centrally coordinated fashion below.

"It is now time for me to direct my energies towards our current world affairs," the Mystic King had continued, "addressing problems in both a more spiritual and tangible manner. Our initial modest effort, Operation: Restore Spirit, has already made an impact, reducing violent crime in our cities by nearly two thirds in its first year..."

Who did he think he was? Sure, all musicians write about changing the world, but they stuck with writing and left messing the planet up to the politicians. Musicians *needed* the world to be messed up. And all Nathaniel could think about was that at this point he did not give a shit if the world went to Hell in a hand basket.

My name is Nathan!

Jesse...

Now there was someone who wanted to change the world. And if he had had the chance to do it, Nathan would have been right there with him, and happy to be a part of it. But here—almost ironically—the world *was* actually getting better, safer. Wasn't it?

So why am I so unhappy?

The truth could not escape Nathan; his life was exactly how he had wanted it, and he could not be more miserable. He craved nothing more than a final release from this existence.

"Who do you love?"

A stiff breeze kicked up, and instead of fighting it, Nathan closed his eyes and allowed his body to lean forward...

Citations

Chap	Reference
	Tolkien, J.R.R. *The Silmarillion*. Balantine Books, 1990.
1	Eliot, Thomas Stearns. *The Hollow Men*, *Poems: 1909-1925*, T.S. Eliot, 1925.
3	Nietzsche, Friedrich. (1844-1900).
7	Plato. (427 B.C.-347 B.C.).
8	Milton, John. (1608-1674). *Paradise Lost* (bk. XI, l. 414), 1667.
10	Hugo, Victor-Marie. (1802-1885).
11	Fox, Charles & Gimbel, Norman. *Killing Me Softly* (as recorded by Roberta Flack, Atlantic/Wea, 1972).
14	Casals, Pablo. (1876-1973).
19	Thoreau, Henry David. (1817-1862). *The Service*, 1840.

For additional information on authors, artists, works, and quotes cited in *Dominion* (including the ability to purchase) please visit www.thedominionproject.com/citations.html .

The Dominion Project continues with Book V

ASCENSION

Fettering Star

With the power of music at his back, Jimi T. Expo steps onto the political landscape with a singular purpose, to draw all peoples and nations together for the glorious transition into the next age. The collapse of a one-time superpower sends the entire planet into a third world war, drawing the Mystic King in to broker a peace agreement before a nuclear exchange takes place. One man, Sir Thomas Leese, remains Jimi T.'s sole political adversary, yet will his 'loyal dissent' only hinder the world's one chance to avoid a real Armageddon? Father Daniel Ananias, his final calling revealed, embarks on a one-way mission with an ill-fated task; offer the world's new Messiah a choice…

Direct Ordering of the Dominion Series

Especially for those who do not have online access, all books can be purchased direct from T.C.C./Sacrata Dei Press by mail.

Dominion – The Series

Book I: Seed	*(June 2009)*
Book II: Phoenix	*(July 2009)*
Book III: Tryst	*(August 2009)*
Book VI: Requiem	*(October 2009)*
Book V: Ascension	*(December 2009)*
Book VI: Abyss	*(May 2010)*
Book VII: Revelation	*(January 2011)*

Dominion – Reference

For the Dominion reading enthusiast who wishes to delve deeper into the series, these brief reader's companions/reference are a helpful tool providing character profiles, time and location references, summaries, background, and descriptions. Each Interlude is meant to follow its corresponding book from the series, offering a more in-depth understanding of the "Dominion world" while further preparing the reader for the next book.

First Interlude
Second Interlude
Third Interlude
Fourth Interlude
Fifth Interlude
Sixth Interlude
Coda: Deux Ex Machina

Please call (574) 307-0413 for current mailing address, shipping rates, and tax rates (where applicable). Once obtained, please identify in your mailing your name and address, which book(s) you are ordering and the quantity, and provide a check or money order in U.S. dollars made payable to T.C.C./Sacrata Dei Press.

www.ingramcontent.com/pod-product-compliance
Lightning Source LLC
Chambersburg PA
CBHW022153260626
47155CB00018B/1866